GRAAL FLIBUSTE

ROBERT PINGET

GRAAL FLIBUSTE

A NOVEL

TRANSLATED BY ANNA FITZGERALD

DALKEY ARCHIVE PRESS

The publication of this work was not supported in any way by CNL (Centre National du Livre), the French government agency that exists to promote the translation of French literature through partial and minimal financial support. Dalkey Archive Press protests such mistreatment of translators and will cease publishing French literature until this abuse stops.

Originally published in French by Les Éditions de Minuit, Paris, 1966
Copyright © 1966 by Les Éditions de Minuit
Translation copyright © 2014 by Anna Fitzgerald

LIBRARY OF CONGRESS CATALOGING-IN-PUBLICATION DATA

Pinget, Robert.
 [Graal Flibuste. English]
 Graal Flibuste / by Robert Pinget ; translated by Anna Fitzgerald. -- First edition.
  pages cm
 Originally published in French by Éditions de Minuit (Paris), 1956.
 Summary: "This early work by the landmark Swiss author Robert Pinget is unlike any other he produced over his long career; indeed, there are few books by any writer with which it bears comparison--aside perhaps from the novels of Raymond Roussel or Denis Diderot. Graal Flibuste follows the progress of its narrator and his impudent coachman, Brindon, through a fantastical land peopled by strange creatures and stranger potentates, and filled with tall tales, mysteries, crimes, dilemmas, and deities ... not least among whom is the terrible god Graal Flibuste himself" -- Provided by publisher.
 ISBN 978-1-62897-112-5 (pbk. : alk. paper)
 I. Fitzgerald, Anna, translator. II. Title.

 PQ2631.I638G713 2015
 843'.914--dc23
                          2015017339

Partially funded by the Illinois Arts Council, a state agency.

www.dalkeyarchive.com
Victoria, TX / London / Dublin

Cover: Typesetting and layout by Arnold Kotra
Composition and art by Jeffrey Higgins

Typesetting: Mikhail Iliatov

Printed on permanent/durable acid-free paper

CONTENTS

GRAAL FLIBUSTE

A drunk sits at a table, facing a bottle. He wears a hat, his nose is red, and his eyes are lost in contemplating things. He asks himself why he's there and shrugs his shoulders. From time to time he gestures half-heartedly with his forearm.

The cat thinks his master stupid for not having drowned him yet. He's hideous and smelly, and his head's so big he can hardly move. We're a good match, thinks the cat. I'm a ridiculous monster and he's a nobody, which amounts to the same thing.

The drunk refills his glass and drinks. He looks up and sees the cat perched on the shelf. What a useless shelf, thinks the drunk. I've got nothing to put on it but that cat. He balls up a bit of bread and throws it at the animal, who gulps it down. Having forgotten his first throw, the drunk makes another ball and tosses it. The cat gulps that down too, then moves to the stove, which is always cold. At least he can't reach me here, thinks the cat, since he's incapable of turning around.

The drunk refills his glass and drinks. He no longer sees the cat on the shelf and wonders where he's gone. He starts thinking he might have swallowed him with his wine. Such is the reasoning of a drunk. I must have swallowed that cat, now I'm all alone. Reminded of his solitude, the drunk begins to weep.

The cat decides the stove is uncomfortable after all and goes back to the shelf.

The drunk refills his glass and drinks.

The cat begins to groom himself out of boredom. His big head tips further and further, he can no longer hold it up and falls to the ground. The drunk hears him fall. He thinks the cat wants to kill him. When he makes a sudden move, the cat in turn thinks the drunk wants to kill him. He jumps on the stove.

The drunk throws up. That's it, it's over, thinks the cat, he'll give me my dinner soon if all goes well. But some nights, nothing goes anywhere, thoughts and movements get trapped in a cul-de-sac. It seems to me there are more and more nights like this as we age. Then, one fine day, as if someone forgot to wind a clock, we end up at some dead-end hour of the night before, having died in our sleep.

The ceiling begins to descend. A battle, thinks the drunk. They're fighting for the whites, I'm red. I've already lost. Stand back! The canons are on the other side, the sea will drown the cat, the enemy, what's he got in his mouth, my letter, he'll destroy it, swallow it, my only letter, come a little closer so I can wring your neck, the letter I was waiting for, the letter the whites don't believe in any longer. So much time, so much time, and all this wine, over account of a letter that never arrived . . . Sailor, tell me if the letter made it, it's soaked through and through, deep in your pocket, nothing in the world besides that cat at my heels means more to me than this letter, flowing with the current.

The drunk falls asleep on the table and is transported by the wine to a land littered with the cadavers of letters. Many letters never reach their destination; they wait in post offices, then the angel of letters assassinates them. This is love's enemy, a desiccated angel with paper wings.

THE TEMPLE

Chanchèze is a dismal valley populated by rats. The road there is flanked by piles of rocks. Near the middle of the valley stands the temple of Graal Flibuste.

Desolation and fetor. The ground is strewn with the cadavers of rats, their skeletons crunch underfoot. The temple stands amid this carrion. It resembles a casino. People of my generation find the baroque architecture of its façade and its tasteless ornaments amusing. It was noble in its day. From its pediment, an enormous bowel uncoils onto the architrave, rounds the capitals, and rises up to the roof, crowning it with a sort of intestinal shrubbery. Bizarrely veined with red near the top, the columns are black and lumpy like burned-out lava from the middle down. Birds with long beaks nest in the holes; at sunset, when they return home, the columns bristle like the stems of a wild rosebush. These birds are said to feed on rats. But according to Porphyreus, they are not carnivorous; they merely kill the rodents. To obtain their food, they fly great distances to the Forest of Grance. The mothers then return to regurgitate the wild fruit and bark they've ingested into the beaks of their young.

No rats can be seen on the temple steps, and the birds never alight there; the reason for this has yet to be discovered. Legend has it that Graal Flibuste, defender of banks, lays a curse on any living being that touches the sanctuary floor.

The interior is decorated with paintings whose basic motif is a sort of peanut shape, a double ovoid figure. The elegance inside the temple, of which the exterior gives no hint, comes as a surprise. The ceiling, a black and white checkerboard, is painted to imitate a game of chess with trompe-l'oeil pieces. A small altar occupies the center of the temple. Enormously heavy, it has sunk into the floor by about a third of its height.

On the left, the wall supports a kind of sacristy or stall closed off by a thin partition. The entrance is too low to pass through without stooping. Inside, very few of the ceremonial accessories still remain, aside from a scrap of tapestry and a trowel used for symbolic plantings.

The sadness of the temple, where neglect has taken on a strange density, quickly disheartens the visitor. He returns to the parvis, where the stench of the mass grave threatens to strangle him.

THE PALM GROVE

The Sultan, upon learning I was in the vicinity, extended an invitation. He dwelt in the heart of the country's most beautiful palm grove, rumored to have cost the lives of some ten thousand men during the irrigation work; they perished under the whip, the master deeming their yield insufficient.

I rented a carriage with a tattered opulence, trimmed with painted arabesques and silk curtains. The decrepit seat was slowly losing its stuffing, made from a sort of kapok called bouri-bouri, the fluffy seed of the carnivorous plant known as stuk.

I positioned myself in the carriage, on the right side of the bench, and bid my coachman to be off.

My coachman cut a fine figure. Massive, broad-shouldered, with the head of a god and small ears. His neck was admirable, as wide as two hands and dotted with impressively black acne. He wore a cavalier's hat with a violet plume that had slipped against his shoulder. The buttons on his imperial guard vest were mismatched and his open shirt revealed a beadle's chain on a hirsute chest. I might speak of his nose, but he didn't have one. A war injury, from a cannonball or saber blade, had divested him of it. His mouth was sensual and his eyes like two truffles tucked into the canned pork of his cheeks. His gaze flowed with malice over a walrus mustache, giving him the look of those diplomats wearied by revelry that one sees at the conference tables of young democracies.

The horse was a jaundiced shade of gray and didn't measure up to his master, but he trotted along cheerfully enough. The ride was quite jarring. My coachman kept turning to announce the presence of yet another pothole and took pleasure at my pained expression.

What grand country we were traversing! The suburban regions were sprinkled with islets of market gardening, along a stream where tiger-birds and guinea pigs splashed about. The desert died out there as the last grains of sand rose up in occasional swirls, which my coachman compared to dancers. In the familiar parlance of the natives, this phenomenon is called the "farts of Abraham." To the right, rosy hills stretched into the distance, planted with lollipop vines and large catalpas. To the left, just beyond a stretch of scant vegetation, one could make out the incipient splendors of the desert. And a few leagues ahead of us, the green line of the palm grove.

I asked my coachman whether the hundreds of thousands of guinea pigs I saw frolicking around the river lived free or had been bred. "Both," he replied. "Or rather, the domesticated and wild variants are now indistinguishable. The biggest landowners have developed the 'gipi' on their estates, and its eminently sociable qualities attract all the non-domesticated variants that swarm over the region. The herd you're seeing now has scarcely moved from this spot over the last three years. It started with one hundred odd gipis from the royal stables. Consider the profit this represents . . ."

But the tiger-birds had captured my attention. Tawny brown with blue stripes, comparable in size to swans, they muck through the river-edge silt, chase each other into the gorse bushes, and let out horrendous roars as they fly from bank to bank—hence their name. The racket is deafening. These are sacred birds. With their wings outstretched, they resemble vampires, but they are gentle sorts and live in harmony with the guinea pigs, who in turn protect the birds from parasites. The main parasite of the tiger-birds is the "mange-mange" spider, which flees at the mere scent of a guinea pig. Should a peasant kill a bird-tiger when food is scarce, he is obliged to purify himself in the river that very day and make an offering of his victim's heart and gizzard to Graal Flibuste. I had been unaware that the solitary god reigned over these parts, and the realization filled me with gloom; everything I'd learned so far about Graal Flibuste evoked sad scenes or desolate junctures. Perhaps it was the desert's proximity, more than the tiger-birds, that prompted my guide to mention the god.

The beauty of the landscape intensified. Already the first

palm trees surrounded us. Their trunks are twice as thick as a cedar's, perfectly smooth, and mahogany in color. They soar fifty yards from the ground and then burst into a tuft of blue and violet palms intertwined with flowering vines of saffron clematis. I was enchanted by this natural exuberance. Black carnations and emerald centauries carpeted the ground, exuding a sweet fragrance. Everything invited gentle dozing, voluptuous dreaming. I bid my coachman to slow our pace, but he urged his horse onward, either fearing the advancing hour or under orders not to let foreigners stop in these parts. I no longer felt the slightest bump; the ground was pastureland and my seat a plush bed. I relished the swoon of my well-being. Before long we were deep in the palm grove.

A vine fell from a tree and landed on my knees. What I'd taken for clematis were in fact tiny human figures. Their minuscule mouths were humming something. I leaned in to hear.

You haven't yet loved
The only thing lovable,
Seek in the palm grove
The answer most ideal.

As I passed from mouth to mouth, each one singing the same words at alternate times, I was transfixed by their melodious fugue. I expressed my surprise to the coachman, who burst out laughing. The liana promptly rotted in my hands. A glutinous larva emerged, which I tossed from the carriage. No sooner had it touched the ground than an immense palm tree towered overhead.

THE BUTTERFLY-MONKEYS

"We've arrived," the coachman announces.

I step out of the carriage onto the ground. The vegetation is so luxuriant that my head begins to swim. The coachman offers his arm and we walk a few paces toward the palace, which emerges from behind a jumble of plants, water jets, and darting butterfly-monkeys. The animals fly or leap from one hedge to the next, their multicolor wings like cashmere and their tails tracing elegant scrolls. They come from the Île of Phul, imported two centuries ago by explorers who also left behind a curious legend.

The coachman tells me that, according to this legend, a band of brigands known as the *Perciflails* or *Percifalls* or *Perciwails* left their islands once upon a time to raid these parts. Three of them tried to abscond with the royal monkeys. Thrown into prison, they were rescued by the butterfly Sa-Kur, who was then named generalissimo of the band. Sa-Kur formed a pact with the Sultan, who gave him a monkey to be his bride; she would become mother of the first butterfly-monkeys.

We sit on the edge of a fountain to admire the grace of these creatures. Noticing us, one of them flits our way and begins to twirl and prance around us.

I pick a jolladie and hold it out to the animal. As he eats from my hand, I caress the softest of pelts. A continual shiver runs through his wings, as downy as a moth's; I say this out loud and the animal replies: "Believe me, sir, if you had wings, the fever would never leave you. We are butterflies and monkeys; who can express the sadness of a love with two faces?" He slips free and flies off.

We walk around hedges, along pools. Snakes in nasturtium hues chase each other across the water, skimming past the aquatic peonies. On artificial islets, large bakimpo lilies dotted with cornflowers alternate with so-called "rat-eating" orchids and climbing pulvigeras. Especially fond of pulvigera seeds, the butterfly-monkeys will fight over the tiniest morsel. Flowers and fruit grow simultaneously on the plant, but in autumn the fruit predominates. It is during this period that cameramen try to capture the murderous battles. I saw one of their documentaries and was quite disappointed: Only the eyes and claws of the butterfly-monkeys imprint on the film, and their combat is reduced to a criss-cross of dots and commas on the screen.

Aside from these seeds, the butterfly-monkeys eat vermin and snails. They are not above eating gamy meats or the sap of flowers. "Can they be domesticated?" I asked the coachman.

"Around one in five, but not after their fourth month. They're used to trim the vines."

THE PALACE

We enter the palace. A magnificent patio tiled in blue and gold, birds with purple crests, gracious horse-swans, fake crocodiles. The horse-swans glide across the central pool tossing their manes. They repeat this nervous movement endlessly, neighing all the while. What beauty in their expressions! Those arching necks, those velvety plum-colored ears, those human eyes searching for a mate beyond the walls—an impossibility, since these creatures have been castrated. They are eaten on the feast day of Saint Shezit, the coachman tells me, after being roasted whole in raspberry bushes. The ceramic crocs are jointed and scurry amid the scat of the purple birds. Palm trees arc over the water, then give way to a circular border of quivering coral shrubs. Dreamlike landscape—if only I had my camera to capture you for my albums! A carafus mid-fountain splashes his water jet at beetles in the arabesques.

We sit down on a bench. Behind us, a door veiled with silk. Somewhere a pedantic voice is articulating phrases from a grammar book, interrupted now and again by a woman's tittering laughter.

"That's the Sultana," my charioteer tells me, "she's learning French. She comes from the suburban neighborhoods and I leave you to imagine how her idiom jars the royal milieu."

Straining to hear, I approach the curtain.

But at that moment, out of a doorway steps a black servant who motions us to follow him. Patios, marble parlors, crystal corridors, hanging gardens, bedchambers, and vestibules flow one into the next, and we move through these splendors like tourists no longer susceptible to surprise. Finally, the servant stops in front of a door in carbuncle and chalcedony, incrusted with cement plates.

"Here," he says.

"Here, what?" I ask.

"This is where they've been expecting you for the collation."

No sooner does he press the frame than the door turns on itself and whisks us into the room.

"Be seated," says the servant. "I shall inform His Highness you've arrived."

The prolonged ringing of a bell alerts us to the Sultan's approach. A door opens and chamberlains, valets, and bodyguards emerge, distinguished from each other by the different colors of their pearl-embroidered loincloths. The guards are unarmed except for their phenomenal musculature and their teeth, razorsharp by all appearances. Their torsos are tattooed with hieroglyphic signs to confuse and unnerve attackers.

The headwaiters and valets line up along the wall behind the fully laid-out table; the guards form a hedge. The child with the bell appears and fills the room with its chime, thereby announcing the master's arrival.

His Highness makes his entrance.

At first, only a violet globe can be seen, topped with a golden tree. This is the dressing gown of the Sultan and his ceremonial turban. As he draws nearer, I glimpse his head between the drooping branches of his extravagant headdress. His body, unparalleled in its rotundity, fills the gown like a hay bale. The servants bow, the guards stand at attention. A small hand gracefully emerges from the dressing gown and makes a gesture of welcome in our direction. We kneel to the ground. The Sultan steps forward to bless us, tracing circles above our heads.

"Stand up, gentlemen."

"Sire, although our voyage is unofficial, we pay you the homage of our respective governments."

"I am aware, gentlemen, of the interest your countries take in my kingdom's fortunes, but I suspect their consideration is not without political intent."

A subtle smile played behind the Sultan's mustache as he asked for his handkerchief.

"Excuse me, I drool."

He was indeed drooling. A servant wiped the corners of his mouth. We then moved toward the table and sat down.

Turning to me, our host said, "I do hope that your personal troubles will in no way spoil your pleasure."

I was surprised by this remark.

We took our meal in the oriental manner, conversing all the while.

A STORMY YOUTH

The monarch had led an interesting life. He was the eldest son of the Count of Travail. At birth, he was kidnapped by pirates who took him far from his native land, to the outermost reaches of the province of Lampoilia. These barbarians developed a fondness for the child, who was raised with a heavy hand. At age twelve, he was raped by a henchman, which undermined his nervous system and turned him into the sort of pale, worried adolescent that eventually sinks into vice. He sank. But a madam who put our boy to work in her New Babylonian brothel turned out to be quite generous. She gave him a certain sum that enabled him to travel. The desire to find his family, not uncommon in the disinherited, drove him to scour the western provinces. One day he happened on his younger brother, Gaspard de la Motte, in a family-run hotel in Agapa. Coco—that was the young man's name—could no more boast of his resources than Gaspard. But both had a passion for living and longed to escape the impasse in which they found themselves. They decided to go into business together, borrowing from a spinster to rent a hairdressing shop. Gaspard specialized in hair and Coco in beards. People were soon saying the brothers' fortune would be made when a stupid neighborhood riot put an end to their plans. The shop was ransacked, Gaspard was hung from a hook, and Coco, escaping the mob's fury by the hand of Providence, barely had time to flee to the rooftops. Not knowing where to step, he wandered between earth and sky for a time, as the riot lasted three days. He ate cats he found in the gutters and was finally given shelter in an attic by a maid. This girl, driven to despair by her repulsive face, found in Coco a means to satisfy her repressed yet legitimate needs. He stayed for eight days in the company of his benefactress. She cooked for them on an alcohol stove, concocting delectable dishes of pork and beans. But her employer, a certain Marquise Pleure-Beignet, caught them one night in the stairway. She dismissed her servant, and Coco found himself out on the street again. Marie tried to detain him, saying she knew of a place where they could both find work, but Coco was not unhappy with this chance to leave. He ditched his kind friend on the spot, wishing her prosperity of every sort. Then he took the first train, this time heading east. In the compartment, he made the acquaintance of a military officer returning to his unit who invited Coco to get off at the little station in Chatruse, close to the barracks. They settled on a deal that was scarcely equitable and plunged Coco back into depravity; but the remuneration of certain generals, said the mercenary, would assure him a decent existence and even the possibility to set aside a little money. They got off the train together, Coco took up residence at the inn, and the officer informed him when his first appointment would be. The following day, at eight in the evening, the officer came around to see the boy with a general and two sergeants.

Coco remained in Chatruse only as long as was needed to replenish his coffers. Then, one lovely evening, he set out alone, heading east again. A string of adventures led him to Vadroliapolis, where fortune smiled on him. In a movie theater, he caught the eye of an old lady, his neighbor, who found him quite to her taste. As they walked out, Coco could not have been more surprised to find a chauffeur waiting for them. In a massive car, with heraldic arms on the doors.

He questioned his benefactress. She was none other than a former flame of the Count of Travail. A few weeks later, the old lady legally adopted Coco and made him her heir. The other relations they had were in no way governed by contract. Coco was as spoiled as could be. His adopter breathed her last breath two years later, having received the sacraments from her church. Coco married the daughter of the Sultan who, having no male heirs, left Coco his kingdom. Coco became Sidi, and there you have the story.

THE SORCERER'S WOE

By our means of transport, we journeyed to the land of rootless trees. They position themselves at nightfall and mimic forests or clearings, but should a garter snake slip through the grass, they flee, becoming no more than rushes, then wrinkles on the surface of the lakes. The big lakes of Grance, that is.

"My land is arid," said the sorcerer, "and I am powerless to give it water. My land is thirsty, the desert is invading, the orchards are shriveling, the stone is showing through the soil. Why bother to change the sky into an army of frogs, or men into pumpkins, or beasts into gravel. My powers are trivial."

As the sorcerer wept, the lakes took shape around him. Soon he was on a little island that would come to be called the Island of Woe. It abounds with flowers that soothe liver troubles, in remembrance of the bilious sorcerer.

We pitched our tent on the shore of a lake. It was evening, and the petroleum on the water gleamed like silk moiré. Eels sped across the surface emeralds in flashes of opalescence. A beautiful landscape, but sad. A feeling of peril. Would any of this still be here tomorrow, would our laundry, washed in great haste, not fly away with the trees? I had very few undergarments. My coachman assured me that we could procure drawers and handkerchiefs in the textile cooperatives, but I wasn't counting on it. Besides, how would we pay? Two of our suitcases had been stolen in the palm grove, leaving us with nothing to barter. We did have our shoes, but my feet were a bit sensitive at the time. As for the rest of it, we didn't trouble ourselves, surrounded as we were by nature. I remember my need to speak of cities; I had fallen prey to an urban nostalgia. Memories of our central station, of trains whistling, of the smell of waiting rooms. How paradoxical we are! To the point of wondering why I'd boarded the train last year instead of staying on the platform. This mania for setting off . . .

"Talking to yourself?" the coachman asked.

"I do apologize—train stations again."

"You seem rather tired to me. Here, I've prepared you this pillow."

The good man had killed a bat, sown the wings together, and stuffed the inside with leaves and aromatic plants. He had an ulterior motive, however; he planned to recover his gift the following day and cook it, as we were out of victuals. But I won't mention his peculiar beignets.

"Life is strange," I said. "Nothing but chance encounters and disappointments."

"How true!"

"Being dependent on others causes us to lose our independence."

"I beg your pardon?"

"I regret our taking French leave from the Sultan."

"But what a way to dismiss us!"

"Wasn't it, though?"

"And these matters which are immaterial, and our ideal, my dear man . . ."

A herd of elephants passed on the opposite shore. The big lake blackened.

THE BLOUES

After a few months of camping and hunting, we grew tired of the region. Entertainment was scarce. Brindon—that was my coachman—complained that I lacked imagination. I had indeed drawn up a timetable to which I adhered as closely as possible, since I find leisure pernicious. Up at eight, I would wash by the water's edge, then swim for two hours, either moving along the shore or crossing the lake from end to end. I forced myself through this exercise. The crossing was especially irksome, as the depths seemed to harbor abysses and whirlpools and who knows what treacherous forces that might pull me down without a trace. I like my mysteries comfortable or not at all. To dissuade me from entering the water, Brindon recounted all the stories he knew of drownings, inundations, monsters, and shipwrecks. The tales about our lake became more and more numerous. I noted this with irony, but was eventually convinced. Stupidity and patience go hand in hand, a force to be reckoned with. I soon abandoned crossing the lake, then swimming along the shore, and very nearly gave up splashing myself with a little water on the beach. At around ten o'clock, in the days before my defeat, I'd emerge benumbed from the lake and run a few hundred yards on the elephant track, as flat as a croquet field. Then I'd make my way back and dress. Brindon would just be waking up. His mouth still pasty, he'd demand his eggs and ants. I'd break four eggs and scramble them in a pan with a pound of these insects. They were precious to us. We collected them in the evening by candlelight. After breakfast, Brindon went back to sleep and I went hunting. I took a stick and set out for the rock piles where the bloues nest. Originally from Chanchèze, these animals abound in the lake region. They are absolutely harmless and have no impulse to flee. I could dispatch the two bloues necessary for a day's rations in short order.

Similar in size to a rabbit, the bloue is covered in velvety beige fur. Its spindly neck is hairless and up to eight inches long. Its head is minuscule and resembles that of a turtle. With its long claws, it can scamper up the steepest rocks. Its flesh is tender and cooks in a few minutes.

Here's a family of bloues stretched out in the sun. I home in on the mother and father. Waving my stick as lightly as a wand, I fell each one in turn. The youngsters I'll save for next week; they're milling around the cadavers. Be gone, you little rascals. I push them into an anfractuosity with my hand. Some neighboring mother bloue will come around to feed them; within a few days they'll plump up to adult size and their soft fur will grow in. Strange creatures! I enjoy remembering the mornings I wandered alone and aimless among these flocks like a good shepherd, who chooses his victims and leaves nature to rectify his crimes. The gods who protect us have no other duty, and we're cowardly enough to seek their favor.

The mother in one pocket, the father in the other, I tranquilly return to our camp, making a detour by the shrubland. Giant patches of broom shade the ferocious lettuce that makes such tasty salads. It is not uncommon for half-digested larvae to still be writhing in the plant's stomach when I hand my harvest to Brindon.

Pink broom, purple broom, arborescent formulaya, mauve piquedule, simple snowballs, wild rose, the enchanting scent of oraltize and rogonoue—variety is endless on the Grance Savannah! I weave through the shrubs observing the fauna, limited to reptiles and small saurians. I remember one morning when I came across a kind of chameleon trying to crawl along an oraltize stem. Straightening the stem and pushing the lizard, I managed to help him up. He said to me: "Sir, you are a friend to nature, thank you. You understand the needs of poor animals. But let me warn you: This type of sensibility cuts both ways. The more compassion you show your inferior brothers, the less you will appreciate your fellow man. I'm speaking against myself, against the entire animal kingdom, because of the profound respect I have for you."

These words upset me but I gave no sign of my feelings. Continuing with my walk, I gathered flowers and brought back a dazzling bouquet for Brindon. He received me coldly.

DIVAGATION

Having set off once again, we let the horse trot along. I'd noticed a certain independence in this animal. A blind will drove him, to what end I can't say, and made him indefatigable. Brindon, who knew his horse and was not inclined to metaphysical considerations, paid this no heed, but how many times did he brace against his seat rein in Clotho, who never wanted to stop.

The track cut through the shrubland, where the broom was redder than ever. Like a bloody wave it swept all the way to the horizon. The gentle landscape I spent my mornings botanizing seemed suddenly hostile, our outfit less solid, our terms less certain. We were leaving again, I said to myself, always leaving again, why? But then, destiny toys with our uncertainties and seems most foreign in the moments we become fully aware of ourselves.

Drifting somewhere between sleep and wakefulness, I amused myself by composing the preface of an imaginary book: "I was born in a desert, near a fountain that disappeared whenever we were thirsty. My parents knew how to live on their reserves, which I'd almost grown accustomed to when a

caravan snatched me from their tender care and brought me
to a land where a thousand fountains sprang up at the mere
thought of thirst. In short, I never found a balance between
right and 'in the red,' as accountants say. This colored my character with a sort of mistrust that deprived me over the years of
what strengthens others: experience. I've progressed backward,
so to speak, so that I'm now as helpless as a newborn. I intend
to postpone, in choosing to write, the death sentence I must
lay on my own head, but let the reader be warned that this
book, like the author's life, grows more and more meaningless
the longer it becomes, contrary to custom . . ."

THE CERAMICISTS

"Well, get out already," Brindon said to me. I'd drifted off to
sleep. Where were we? Apparently in a village square, but I was
only half-awake . . .

"Watch the step, it broke along the way."

"Where are we, my dear man?"

"Never mind, someplace I'll be able to sleep."

He's out of sorts, I thought. No use insisting. A figure helped
him to unhitch Clotho, but I couldn't make out any features
in the dark. I gathered up what remained of my belongings:
a little toiletry kit, a knitted beige blanket, and the umbrella. I didn't dare question Brindon and tried to find my own
way. In front of me, three small lights at ground level: hurricane
lanterns shining on the steps of three stairways. Three identical doors, three adjoining houses. Their pointed roofs stood
out against the sky. On the left, further along, three lanterns,
three houses, three gables. Likewise on the right, and behind
me. Likewise all around. Yes, a village square, I saw the fountain and the war memorial now. But what a curious arrangement! The space between each trio of houses made the square
seem immense. Finally some organized people, I said to myself.
People to chat and relax with, nothing bizarre to worry about.
Leaning on my umbrella, the blanket draped about my shoulders, I enjoyed the honest pleasure of calm surroundings, fresh
air, and a sky much like our own, with little clouds scudding

by. Brindon and his helper had finished unhitching. They left the carriage on the square. Brindon's instructions as he pulled at Clotho's bridle: "Follow us." A stopover he knows, I thought; so much the better. Eventually the unexpected gets old.

We led the horse to a stable behind the complexes. Very clean and well lit, it seemed more like a washhouse than a stable. Refinement had been taken to an extreme; the native explained that the cows were shod in felt slippers to prevent any hoof marks on the floor. Outside each stall was a glass countertop with a toothbrush and a tumbler. The dental hygiene of cows has significant repercussions on their lactic capacities. Our guide readily admitted that the ruminants were not yet able to care for their teeth themselves, but his pride was undeniable as he showed us the bathroom and lavatory (his euphemistic name for the water closet), where the animals had been trained to bathe and relieve themselves. The kind of wet bar one finds in American homes was installed in a corner of the stable; our friend served us glasses of ice-cold milk.

I made a detailed description of our host's physique. He had a face one would call open, with ruddy features, blue eyes, blond hair, a large build, an embroidered vest, fustian pants—something Tyrolean, overall, though we were far from those peaceful mountains. His name was Kruk or Krukr. We followed him into the house. On the ground floor, a common room, tastefully furnished and entirely painted with little flowers. The dishes that filled the hutch were decorated with flowers, the curtains were printed with flowers. Kruk excused himself and went to the kitchen to improvise a meal; his wife was already in bed at that late hour. I took the opportunity to ask Brindon what sort of people our hosts were, and the villagers in general. "The natural sort," he replied. That should be fine, I was thinking, until Kruk brought us milk soup accompanied by yogurt and double cream. I can't stand milk. The conversation focused on the latest ravages of foot-and-mouth disease, the diverse uses for whey, and the advantages of milk cooperatives. I fell asleep on my flowered chair until the next morning, when I was awakened by a light tap on the shoulder. It was the amiable Kruk, holding out a glass of milk. Brindon appeared at that moment and hurried me along. We were late for our visit to the ceramic workshops.

I was hardly looking forward to this visit. I imagined that some sort of cheesemaking practice would be involved, and felt ill in advance. What happened next proved me wrong, as we shall see.

The workshops were about a mile away and we went by foot. Brindon explained that we were going for my sake, since he wasn't much of an art enthusiast. He sketched out a rather basic theory of aesthetics, decrying anything that didn't meet the standards of utility. My interest grew as we approached the artists' refuge. This milk-rich diet shows promise, I said to myself, because contrary to expectation . . .

And here we were. A simple shack of corrugated steel. We went in. "What does the gentleman desire?" asked the doorman. And that's all. There was nothing, nothing, nothing.

DESIRE

How their lovers must suffer when those gifted in the arts of the flesh suddenly abandon this world and dedicate themselves to some pious pursuit or lofty dream. For no worship is more ardent than that of sensual pleasure. As if the secret of this art, by revealing itself to its victims, condemns them to seek nothing in life but the indulgence of their passion, while they jealously maintain deep within their bodies its perilous enigma. From the body, the serpent slips into the soul and transmutes lover into visionary. With every step, at every turn in the road, he sees the object of his desires . . .

This is what befell Monsieur Songe. I told my coachman the story for his amusement.

It was at a neighborhood dance that Monsieur Songe met Mademoiselle Hortensia. To imagine him in this situation, a few details are required. An old dodderer, he only goes out for half an hour each day, after lunch. He takes rue des Casse-Tonnelles, turns the corner before the grocer's and heads down rue Gou. At that hour, there's practically no one about. Only the laundress nods to Monsieur Songe as she lingers outside her door with Madame Chinze; he responds with ceremony. Madame Chinze never fails to whisper: "The smell of that old celibate turns my stomach." The culprit reaches the end of the street and rounds the corner before the Swan Café. On alternating days, he goes in and orders a marc from Cyril. The faubourg's youth are gathered around the slot machine or playing a game of billiards before they return to work. Someone recounts last night's match between Fantoine and Agapa. By a quarter to two, everyone's gone except for the old ruminant and Cyril, who's drying the glasses. The manageress dozes in her room.

"Out for a walk, Monsieur?"

"Yes indeed, Cyril. One needs the airing out . . . careful or you'll break that glass."

But Cyril is handy and never breaks anything. In time we'll return to this swarthy crowd-pleaser, also a champion basketball player.

Monsieur Songe slips a hand into his vest pocket, takes out his wallet, and pays for his marc. He leaves. Cyril watches him all the way to the creamery, then settles back into his thoughts.

Monsieur Songe has finished his walk, he goes home. The handle of the carriage gate is a sculpted sea-maiden, and the solitary man slides his fingertips slowly over its curves. He then opens and closes his mailbox. Climbing the stairs, he thinks he's been forgotten by So-and-So, an office mate and also his billiards partner. "He must be dead," reckons Monsieur Songe as he changes into his slippers. He sits down at his desk and takes up his report to the committee of former bank employees at Fyfe and Company. A long report that he will never finish.

His encounter with Mademoiselle Hortensia is so at odds with what we know of this character that the meddling of some prankster or Madame Chinze's irony will, I think, be necessary to bring it about. The facts are as follows: On a Monday in October, after passing the grocer's, Monsieur Songe was accosted by a woman in black who said she had something to tell him concerning his brother. "I saw him two months ago," she added, "in Samba-Pescador. He asked that I transmit a dossier to you concerning your inheritance. I've been trying to find you since I arrived. Providence must have arranged this meeting."

With no thought to the improbability of her introduction, Monsieur Songe followed the woman to a honky-tonk where she plied him with beer and cognac late into the evening. He inquired about his brother's life and times in Samba.

"Prosperous indeed," says the woman. "The pasta outfit he bought three years ago is turning a handsome profit. Cadillac, manservant, race horses."

"Has he aged?" asks Monsieur Songe. "Does he look well, is his liver still bothering him?"

"Not at all. He's in perfect health. Every year he goes away for his circulation treatment, simple as that. You know he's divorced from his first wife?"

"Divorced? Horrors. Mother would have never approved . . ."

"Rest assured, his ex . . . What was her name again?"

"Anna."

"Precisely. Anna died shortly after the divorce. Your brother was remarried in the church, and Bertha makes him happier than he ever hoped to be at his age."

From here things get hazy. Monsieur Songe loses track and allows himself to be cajoled by the woman, who is in fact a whore. She leads him upstairs, undresses him, and stretches him out on the bed. She tries to reignite what age and alcohol have extinguished, then gives up. She rings for a chambermaid and asks her to keep watch over the client so he won't leave the following day without first seeing her.

"I'll be here at nine o'clock. If he wakes up before then, tell him whatever you like, but persuade him to wait for me."

Monsieur Songe wakes up the next morning at eight o'clock. He is distraught. He can't recall what happened. At half past eight the chambermaid, who happens to be in the hallway, opens the door a crack and sees our man awake. She quietly closes the door and knocks.

"Come in," he says.

"How is Monsieur? Did Monsieur sleep well? Monsieur was very unwell last night."

"Tell me what happened, I can't seem to collect my wits."

"Monsieur was struck by a car last night and brought here. Monsieur was examined by a doctor, he has no bruises, and can leave at nine o'clock. A woman who witnessed the accident will come by to see how he's doing. If Monsieur wouldn't mind waiting for half an hour."

At nine o'clock, a friend of the woman in black arrives and knocks on the door. She explains to Monsieur Songe that an extremely important matter concerning insurance must be resolved at half past ten, and that he is required to attend, and that she would be happy to accompany him.

"I'll wait for you downstairs," she says on her way out.

Monsieur Songe gets dressed. He finds the woman in the café and they leave together. Suddenly Monsieur Songe has a flash of memory. He turns abruptly toward the woman and stares at her.

"No, no," she says. "I'm not the one you spoke to last night. But you'll see her again in a little while."

MANEUVER AND MORALITY

Monsieur Songe found himself utterly drunk that night at Pipon's, the faubourg's bar. It was the feast of Saint Charles and people were dancing in the back room. The hairdresser's assistant, Culot, on the accordion, and Mademoiselle Destrange, on the piano, churned out a waltz. Monsieur Songe sank into despondency on his lawn chair. Madame Fine and Mademoiselle Hortensia helped Pipette wash glasses and prepare sandwiches. The youngsters were having a fine time, pawing at each other honestly, slapping each other's backsides. What could be sadder than the gaiety of common people?

From time to time, Mademoiselle Hortensia glanced toward the lawn chair. She saw retirement, a little house, and the first pew of the church.

"You should go over there and keep him company," said Madame Fine.

"Should I?" asked Mademoiselle Hortensia.

"Sure, go ahead."

"But he's three sheets in the wind, Madame Fine. He can barely hold his head up."

"All the more reason. Don't miss your chance, it's now or

never."

Mademoiselle Hortensia hesitated. Madame Fine untied the younger woman's apron and pushed her in the direction of the lawn chair.

It was morning when Monsieur Songe sobered up, after a brief sleep. He was still sitting in his chair, with Mademoiselle Hortensia holding his head. Her face leaning over him when he awoke was his first revelation of love.

They continued to see each other, communing in the young woman's boudoir. There they contributed the small measure that remained to them of actual grace. This endeavor, whatever it entailed, stirred the old lover's dormant imagination; obsession soon took hold. He became a sordid buffoon, as can happen at that age. Mademoiselle Hortensia laid out her conditions, ten percent went to Madame Fine. Then came the notarized agreement and the wedding.

After a month of conjugality, Madame Songe picked a fight with her husband, convinced a judge of his wrongs, and obtained a divorce in her favor. Monsieur Songe went bankrupt and had to return to work as a night watchman; Madame Songe went into exile with her capital and founded a convent of frenzied virgins in the Chanchèze valley. She's said to remain there to this day, high priestess of libido, steeped to the lips in piety.

CLOTHO

Clotho the dappled, bony horse, Clotho the unobtrusive trotter was merely a semblance. I got up the following night (we had stayed with Kruk after my disappointment that morning) and, unable to sleep, went outside. The sky was overcast. At first I walked around the square, plunged in darkness except for the intermittent glow of my cigarette. I went as far as the war memorial and sat on the last step. As I leaned against the Republic, the vanity of it all filled my mind, and with that sadness particular to disheartened insomniacs, I prepared to return to bed when, just behind Kruk's house, a kind of glittering smoke caught my eye, though it was very faint. Fire? No. A phantom fire. Are my glasses fogging over? I wiped my glasses. No, I see something. Not smoke, a vibration, a phosphorescent trembling. Was there some kind of mystery in this dairy-farming town? I slipped off my pedestal, hurried across the square and around the house. The stable! A halo encircled it, an aureole. I moved closer. The door opened by itself and closed after me.

"I've been waiting for you," Clotho said.

And with that, he began to grow and grow. His gray turned yellow, then snow white, then transparent as diamond. His head touched the ceiling, ripping through it as though it were paper; now the roof was just a ruff around his gigantic neck, his body a cathedral and his legs its pillars. A sumptuous tail unfurled and swept through the air. "Clotho!" I stammered. "Stay with me!" I saw his hooves stamping, ready to leave the earth, but Clotho did not fly. Stable, village, and friends disappeared, leaving only this horse shining and triumphant in the night, and my feeble figure rapt in contemplation. His entire circulatory system appeared through the crystal, I could see the heart beating and the arteries throbbing, I could see the veins flowing with blood, which from red had turned to gold, setting the cardinal points ablaze. This was no longer Clotho's life, it was the firmament's, the flux of the world with its billions of stars, universal gravitation. I heard the voice of heaven thunder forth, but how to transcribe its celestial words?

In the valley, the prophet gathered the words and made from them a moral for human purposes:

"If you've lost all passion, then you go with the dead. If you dislike their company, then you should return to your first desire; therein lies your salvation. Take the child by the hand and never let go, be watchful and travel the road together. It will be without end."

GENEALOGY OF GRAAL FLIBUSTE

Bath, the old sovereign goddess of the waters, was visited in a dream by a pelican. Pleasure had eluded her since the captivity of her husband, Gaudecock, lord of islands and mists. The powerful Pontirius keeps him prisoner under a coral reef, in suffocating fumes. Bath awoke surprised, and called on her daughter, the divine Vaoua, to interpret the dream. The meaning of dreams is written at the bottom of the sea, and Vaoua is an expert in this obscure science. "Mother," she said, "you will know a male who will give you numerous sons and daughters." "Will he be of the bird family?" asked Bath. "I cannot tell you more," answered Vaoua. "I can only tell you to withhold nothing from the father of this new generation."

And Bath, one sleepless night, saw the Great Leopard of the Antipodes coming toward her, and together they performed the sweet labors of love. And Bath conceived twelve sons and twelve daughters known as the Ephemerals. The sons have men's bodies and the mottled fur of wildcats. Their arms end in a single claw that they use to hook the masts of ships and sink them; their feet are bales of hay. The daughters have pelican bodies and women's legs. They prowl around marshes and attract frog hunters with their lascivious laughter; the hunters sink into the mud and die, victims of their desire.

The eldest son of Bath and Leopard, who in olden times was known as Chonzo but today is called Plane, seduced one of his sisters, Tifra, and they had three daughters with leopard tails. The Urns, as they are called, preside over work in the fields and unnatural love. Their names are Bi, Ba, and Bo. At night, you can hear them whispering around places of ill repute; in the countryside, they pour dew onto the fields. Plane and Tifra also had three sons known as the Trances. Their necks are made of marble and they have twelve eyes along their spine. Leopard took Linor, the fairest of his three grandsons, as his lover and gave him the Kingdom of Thin Ground, inhabited by the hatter-men and the hassock-men. As for Calott and Frico, they are particularly revered by the Pataphages as the gods of digestion and fashion. Their iconography depicts only the last of the twelve eyes, called the master's eye by confusion with Linor's story. Calott married one of the Ephemerals, the black Myo, who bore him a son, the dwarf Rzwek, who in turn invented headaches and eczema. According to a Transarcidonian legend, Rzwek murdered the moon, which since then has lacked its own light. Rzwek had six wives he selected from among mortals; he chose the first six hours of the day, the sweetest and most productive. Each hour bore him thirty-four sons and thirty-four daughters, all of them immortal. In the little-known province of Dualie, it is said that the dwarf Rzwek accomplished his task imperfectly when copulating with his first wife and that his seed gushed into the Great Void of the Verb, from which the least fortunate poets draw their inspiration. One of Rzwek's sons from the fourth hour, the handsome Deceit, bore the same defect as his great-uncle Linor. He took to the highways and byways of the earth, coupling with all the beggars he met. Then an alchemist revealed to him the secret of homogeniture, and he spawned a wave of offspring who roamed the world in their turn.

Patrona, the twenty-second daughter of the dwarf and the sixth hour, was seduced by Hemichryse, the god of factories and gardens. Pigus relates their tale in book III of the *Satirae Desperatae.* One day, as Patrona was drying off on the grass after her bath, a watercress plant sprouted between her legs and penetrated her so thoroughly that the following day, the maiden gave birth to an infant who was grassy from head to toe. She named him Virtue. Divinely privileged, the child grew up in a few days and immediately showed a liking for country outings and orgies. He resembles the Greek Dionysus in his drunkenness, but unlike Dionysus, Virtue is not a jocular god. A roll in the hay is serious business as he sees it, a view that has made him a solitary and under-appreciated deity. At dusk, he wanders through the suburbs of big cities in search of greenery and repose. The good folk say that if he doesn't find what he seeks, he rapes little suburban girls on the excavation sites for road construction. Since he only strikes in total darkness, flashing lights are installed to keep him away. Virtue is one of the most remarkable figures of this mythology. Certain artists portray him covered with leaves and birds; others append a phallus to his head. For some he is deformed, with guinea-fowl legs and a duck beak, while still others see him as a kangaroo, an animal known for its timidity and extreme lasciviousness. Most artists, however, depict a poor young man with coal-black eyes and a daisy between his teeth. Virtue begat Red, the god of lightning and vengeance, from Gloria, protector of pharmacists. Lacking the omnipotence of thunderous Zeus, Red uses cunning to take advantage of celestial inattention, upsetting the weather during an open-air dance, for example, to avenge his father for missed opportunities. It is commonly believed that Red has the power to paralyze creditors. Should a debtor come under threat, he goes to Red's sanctuary and burns a candle of bloue fat before the altar.

Red begat Corius, Corius begat Brince, Brince begat Pivus-Spotillion from the goddess Bilbie, in all likelihood, though one easily gets lost in conjectures about this union; Where the tradition appears least uncertain is in Lower-Chanchèze or Para-Chanchèze. The natives of these lands have grown bilberries since time immemorial. According to one legend, the god Pilus caught his foot one day in a bilberry root; the plant immediately knotted itself around the divine ankle with immobilizing force. Pilus is the Para-Chancheziott god of rain. In the odes of the old poet Garou, there are continual allusions to the dryness of this land; it can thus be inferred that the climate changed at some point, for reasons unknown. Monsieur Muller, eminent professor of linguistic studies at the University of Agapa, maintains that the roots *pil* and *piv* are identical, both derived from the Indogomorrhean *pis* (wet). This suggests that Pivus-Spotillion and Pilus are one and the same god, a hypothesis confirmed by the fact that Pivus-Spotillion, although not the god of rain, has the ability, among other characteristics, to make mouths water.

Pivus-Spotillion begat the herring Brettey, the monster with an olive-tree head and a cow's tail who raised the sea and flooded the five continents twelve times. Order was re-established each time by a month of the year, which explains the succession of twelve months. This Brettey, not to be confused with the agricultural god Bottay, gave rise to the conflict between the Peazes and the Muddles. He divulged the affair that the Muddle Chta was having with the Peaze Dine; wishing to avenge himself, Chta set out one night to find Brettey. The herring was keeping a young Peaze at his abode who, on that night, occupied the conjugal bed alone. Entirely unable to see, Chta randomly swung his axe and cut the innocent sleeper in two. As he fled, a group of night-walking Peazes stopped him and saw that he was covered in blood from head to toe. They entered the herring's house and discovered their young kinsman, slain. War was declared between the two camps and ended with the annihilation of both sides. All that remains of the Peazes and the Muddles is this dictum: "Bemuddle me and I'll empeazle you," which basically means that in a given situation, faced with the fear of another's commentary, one must take action such that each party not only goes back on initial judgments, but makes spontaneous proclamations to the contrary.

Brettey gave the garter snake Gac five sons and one daughter, nicknamed the Hunchback. This secondary divinity, patroness of pimps and madams, arranged for her brother Kitou to meet the nymph Loristyche during an orgy in the aquatic salons of the herring. Wild Loristyche, as Pigrus referred to her, was the daughter of the goose Pampan and the eel Flu. She had her mother's wings and liver, her father's tail, and the belly of the hippopotamus Chbch, her grandmother. She was raised in the solitude of the Sirancy-la-Louve swamps and at twenty-five was still a virgin, according to legend. The Hunchback snuck into Pampan's abode and persuaded her to send her daughter to see Kitou, bedridden and dying. The nymph was said to be a miracle worker; more than anything else in this world, solitude is subject to both favorable and unfavorable rumors that nearly always entail a degree of superstition. The goose allowed herself to be persuaded, since the Hunchback promised not to let the young woman out of her sight. What was bound to happen happened; the following day Kitou and Loristyche were found asleep in each other's arms beneath a bower of mussels. Loristyche gave birth to the palm tree Drute, endowed with a human trunk and a dog's genitalia. He begat the three Asters, goddesses of dancing and moonless nights: Aga the blond, Ada the brunette, and Ara the redhead. All three have the claws of a thrush in place of feet. A Manse-era funerary stele, found in the lake region, shows them dancing on their father's cadaver, in keeping with Fissou tradition.

Without recourse to any male, Aga gave birth to the god Can, protector of false news, and to the tortoise Jacqui, who married the Mighty Pine. Their union was barren and the tortoise retired to Dualie where she is honored as the goddess Virota, presiding over the launch of ships and the harvest of early plums. In this mythology, a given divinity often has attributions not directly linked in any way, such as labor in the fields and the things of the sea. This is indicative of a turn of mind in the people of this land who, situated as they are, never learned to choose between possible vocations. They practice all of them without mastery. Their sailors did not discover America and their farmers limited themselves to basic crops—no spirit of adventure. To return to the tortoise Virota, out in the country little wood sculptors can still be found who carve her statue in wild cherry wood; children wear these trinkets, devoid of any intrinsic value, around their necks as amulets to ward off unwanted encounters. During our travels in the northern provinces, we documented another custom: The blind carry Virota to avoid *faux pas*. Today the tortoise is enjoying renewed interest from young intellectuals in our cities; this is a fashion that will fade, but may it benefit its followers for as long as the burst of popularity lasts.

The brunette Ada gave birth to twenty-five thousand boys, the Darches. These gods of the air take human form, but are no bigger than a toothbrush tumbler. They nest in trees and steep cliffs. On stormy nights, they can be heard to mewl. Their intentions toward people vary from munificence to malevolence, which makes the population fear them more than all other divinities. At crossroads and in the stairwells of underground urinals, small sanctuaries are built in their honor. According to the poetesse Jeanne, these serve as protection against bad odors, but we consider her interpretation fanciful; the meaning of this custom has been lost in the mists of folklore.

The redheaded Ara gave birth to two daughters, Bar and Chup. The first engendered the horse-swans, which are mortal. The second had a daughter by the god Eguo, nicknamed the Snow Herder; he reigns over the heights with his wife, who shares his favors with Aurora. Eguo is the inventor of malaria and chilblains. His daughter Gentiana, who gave her name to a flower, wanders summit and vale in search of a lover; her putrid breath keeps even the bravest at bay. Before her old husband left her, she conceived Tyrpo, the god of broken hearts. Pursued by the phantoms of his happiness, Tyrpo roams hither and yon like his mother, and laments his fate; in the evenings, he takes the form of a willow's shadow on the banks of ponds, whereas in cities he frequents little cafés and can be heard in the whistling percolators. The son he gave his lover Liana of the Hypermitted Eyes, who died in childbirth, is the famous Gougou. The central figure in this mythology, Gougou is the god of silence. People also say that his mother brought him into this world through her mouth, a consequence of the caprices she had allowed herself with Tyrpo. This led to her inability to speak, which she passed on to her child. There are other stories about this birth; here is the one Verus reported in chapter XV of *Phantasticae Parturitiones*: "When from his birthplace, the Santiar River, the fish Tyrp or Tyrpus arrived at the sea, the crash of the waves was so deafening he took refuge in the depths, ruled by the daughter of Bath and Gaudecock, the mute Mrm (literally, 'cannot even pronounce her own name'). A violent desire overtook him at the sight of this invalid, who commanded her servants with graceful gestures. He offered to marry her. Mrm made it clear she would only accept if he vanquished Pontirius, who held her father captive in his prisons. Tyrp marshaled an army of eels and laid assault to the fortress of Pontirius. But the sea horse sentries it pushed back the assailants and took the fish Tyrp prisoner for venturing onto the battlements. Pontirius spared his life to reward his courage, but nonetheless cut out his tongue. Tyrp returned to Mrm who pardoned his defeat and married him; they had a son they named Gougou because he was mute. He is the god of silence."

Another version of the story is related by Falsus in his *Origines Deorum ac Daemonum secundum historiettas quae audiuntur apud Nauticos*: "The Salamander Tyrpa, daughter of fire and rain, left her underwater abode to escape the threats of the Seal. She set off on a raft, wandered for a thousand years, and reached the kingdom of her father, the beneficent sun. She said to him: 'Father, I am being hunted by the Seal with his pointed teeth, and can find no rest in the sea.' To which the sun replied: 'My daughter, I am to blame for this, having provided you with no means of defense. Henceforth you shall ward off your enemies by breathing fire on them.' And he bestowed her with this power. Tyrpa returned to her deep abode. She found the Seal asleep in her garden. Out of vengeance she breathed fire on him. The Seal was nearly reduced to ashes but did not perish, for he is immortal. His wounds never fully healed, however, leaving his skin spotted with black. He asked for Tyrpa's forgiveness; as penance, the Salamander demanded he found her a spouse. The Seal searched for a thousand years and one day finds the Wind. He brought him to Tyrpa who, delighted by the Wind's puffy face, fell in love with him. Since he has no body, and the Salamander burns everything she touches, their union was purely spiritual; but the power of the mind is such that they had a son, Silence."

Silence begat Idea, Idea begat Speech, Speech begat Discord. This mythology is the only one in the world in which Discord is a benevolent divinity. Discord, in old Chancheziott, is synonymous with freedom regained. She married Tamb, god of music and voyages, who gave her twelve hundred sons in one go. They were raised by their neighbors the Cats, since Tamb and Discord live apart; one travels the world composing operas to be staged by mortals: wars, scientific advances, historical events. The other is so absorbed by her multiple activities that she never goes home. Their children thus learned from the Cats all the tricks and simpering airs of the feline race. Known as the Pewts, they are often confused with their adoptive parents. A Pewt named Honesse seduced an Ephemeral, fat Ida, who conceived Phiss and Jandou. The family's adventures gave rise to a number of fables that H. W. Sampeek collected in a volume entitled *Ida's Mishaps*. People still use the expression "There's a crowd at Ida's," meaning that a scandal is brewing.

The young Phiss, who like her mother had the body of a pelican, gave birth to a series of monsters. It is difficult to identify their father, or fathers; apparently there were several of them, including the bogeymen in that neck of the woods, the Gemps. "I'll hand you over to a Gemp," mothers tell their children.

The offspring of Phiss share the ability to change their appearance. Toat is at times a ram, at times a parakeet with the head of an ass, at times Miljoie Creek, which restores hearing to the deaf, at times the onager Fidelought, invoked by women with cheating husbands. Some deny that Miljoie is a manifestation of Touc, claiming the creek is Pontirius's own son. Chakar, the whippet, becomes Fifty-Footed Boutre on stormy days and Nena in the intimacy of gentle light; in Dualie there is an old prayer to Nena that timid lovers recite before declaring their love. The cunning goddess always answers the supplicant but sometimes changes the beloved into a man if she's a woman, or the opposite. Zelse is a bundle of wood in the morning, a duck-footed pitcher at noon, and a rusty funnel by evening. Ritual is honored in Tranarcie as a brooding turkey; in the province of Fantoine, as an angel with a cornflower head; in Para-Chanchèze, as a wild bore; in the Rouget valley and as far as Sirancy, as a she-wolf, etc. Canabotte (which means "twice born") is the famous Frog from the western provinces and the Blood Grass in the processions of Grance. The giant Mattower, cousin of the Greeks' Atlas, supports the world's weight; he switches it to his other shoulder at the end of winter and becomes a child again, growing as the year advances. Pacta is at times the goddess of harvests, at times ryegrass, at times war; she is depicted on barn doors as a bushel of grain, and on arsenal pediments as a bulldog.

Phiss's brother Jandou is a peaceful being. He invented melody. Like Miljoie Creek, he is also credited with the power to cure the deaf; this superstition provides insight into popular lyricism. During the feast day celebrations held at intervals throughout the year (Soup Day in January, Door Day in March, Leg Day in April-May, Currant Day in June, etc.), processioners carry the god's statue around with a long hose attached that the afflicted hold up to their ears, reciting: "Pan, pan, pan / Open this cave where I hear / The sleepy voice / Of my mother the Echo." In *De Auribus et Organis*, Tropus-Coria relates the story of this miracle from the sixth century: "It was Door Day. The afflicted had turned out in throngs and, accompanied by curious onlookers, they followed in the wake of the god Jandou. When the procession arrived at the place known as Traîne-Misère (the present-day Oublies intersection in Agapa), it was stopped by an unknown force. The statue began to weigh so heavily on the porters' shoulders that they had to put it down. At the sight of these paralyzed men, anxiety began to tighten around the spectators like a vice. But a deaf woman everyone considered mad pushed her way through their ranks and managed to reach the statue. Grabbing the trunk that prolonged the god's mouth, she held it up to her ear and heard the holy words (cf. supra) which she repeated, delirious, to the crowd. Forty deaf people were cured then and there."

With Viola d'Amore, Jandou had a daughter named Tristine, patroness of poor musicians. This goddess, like her distant ancestor the Wind, has no body. She is depicted in the same way that some painters of old depicted cherubs: a face with two wings. Tristine's face is bathed in tears, her wings powdery with ash. In the province of Broy, Tristine is said to have met Tyrpo one evening. The solitary god felt such passion for her that after their union, he cut off her head in a jealous fit. He threw her body into the Santiar River, which turned it into an *île flottante*; this island moves up and down the currents, all the way to the sea where it sometimes disappears for centuries, then suddenly reappears and continues its aimless navigation. Some consider it the Island of Phul, birthplace of the butterfly-monkeys; for others, it is the Island of Woe.

THE DUCREUX

One day as I was flipping through my address book—we had just finished from repairing the axle—Brindon, who was reading over my shoulder, stopped at the entry for Ducreux:

"That name rings a bell," he said. "Who are these Ducreux?"

"Monsieur Ducreux," I replied, "is a wholesaler of cleaning products; a born entrepreneur, he took over his father's operation and developed it considerably. His sanguine temperament thrives on constant activity and the feeling that the world would collapse without him. He gets up at seven o'clock as he has for the last fifty years, he stops by the warehouse at eight o'clock, and by nine o'clock he's sitting at his executive oversized desk like a minister. His secretary, a certain Mademoiselle Nontursac, whose respectable family has fallen on hard times, brings him invoices, orders, correspondence, records, insurance documents—the daily bread of a businessman. He signs, supervises, dictates. Mademoiselle Nontursac always keeps her distance. An extremely well-mannered individual, she's nothing like certain secretaries who readily dominate their employers in the usual way. Mademoiselle Nontursac was presented to Ducreux by an employment agency not known for its probity; one has to wonder why certain institutions continue to insist on their role in our society. They probably represent some deviant form of apostolate, whereby scruples are dispensed with. Mademoiselle Nontursac puts phone calls through to her employer transferred to her by the switchboard operator, a certain Mademoiselle Frip, who was not sent by the employment agency; she was recommended to Ducreux by someone he met in the service named Balloche, who specializes in placing switchboard operators. The said Mademoiselle Frip, whatever her name might suggest, is very pretty, neat, and outgoing. Her nightingale's voice, which keeps callers on the line, is no small asset in a place of business. Ducreux recently gave his operator a raise, whereas Mademoiselle Nontursac continues to live on the wages set five years ago.

"As for Madame Ducreux, she never leaves her apartment. She's a model wife. Brunette at twenty, a redhead at thirty, at fifty her hair was blonde. Her waistline dismays her, but she recently found a dressmaker whose ingenious designs make her appear slimmer. For many years, this former apprentice with Brivance has been dressing the Baroness de Tars who, far from demur, recommended her dressmaker upon meeting Madame Ducreux at the Saint-Firmin parish sale.

"Mademoiselle Ducreux is eighteen. She is not pretty, but her naïve smile lends her a passing charm. She has her father's forehead, slightly bulging, and her mother's noble nose; her skin is that of a redhead and her body like that of a child. 'The engagement will last three years,' decided her mother when Lieutenant Duchemin came around to ask for Gladys's hand in marriage. Madame Ducreux is a Lapive and they have their principles. Originally from Limousin, her family has an exemplary history: Until the Revolution, all the men were gamekeepers in their province; after 1789, they became part of the rural peacekeeping force. A certain Honorin Lapive moved to Paris in 1816, finding work as an archivist for the Keeper of the Seals; his descendents remained in the ministry's employ until the death of Juste Lapive, father of Madame Ducreux.

"'Yes, three years,' continued Madame Ducreux. 'After that we'll have the wedding. In Saint-Firmin or in Limoges, we'll see. Pierre will be working for Father, the two of you will have enough to live on. You'll stay with us for two years, then maybe we'll build something above the warehouses; I've asked Sureau to draw up the plans—four bedrooms, kitchen, and bathroom. You'll need space for the children.'

"The day of her engagement, Mademoiselle Ducreux was pensive, gazing at a pitcher. Her mother remarked: 'Come now, Gladys, a pitcher is a pitcher.' But the mystery of young women is a delicate subject. What was Mademoiselle Ducreux thinking about?"

THE APPLE FOREST

Wild apple trees covered the region. It was autumn, but the trees were barren of fruit; their crimson leaves contrasted with the green of the prairies extending into the horizon. For eight days, we hadn't seen the slightest trace of any inhabitants. The road was overrun by capricious weeds and sometimes barred by a dead tree that obliged us to dismount. The air was extremely pure; the sky's faded blue filled me with familiar thoughts. I was in no hurry to meet people, but the sight of my coachman worried me. He's no longer in his first youth, I thought, which makes his docility all the more touching.

"If we cut across the fields, Brindon, do you suppose we might find something sooner?"

"There you go again with your illogical thinking! Why should these fields be more likely to lead us to a village than the road, however poorly it's maintained?"

"Because a dead road is less reliable than a living prairie."

"I beg your pardon?"

"I didn't say anything."

"What do you mean, you didn't say anything?"

I hadn't opened my mouth. The sentence had come from elsewhere, in a murmur. Brindon wheeled around:

"What's the matter with you? Why don't you answer me?"

"I assure you I didn't say a word."

"It's the hallucinations, they're starting. I doubt our lives will be worth much in a few days."

The road forked at that point, skirting around a thick grove. We both were of a mind to stop and quitted the carriage, leaving Clotho to rest on the side of the road. Once beyond the first curtain of apple trees, I had the impression I'd entered a sanctuary. Not that the trees looked different, not that the relative compactness of their leaves intercepted the light, but somehow the arrangement of space and a certain order inherent in this natural disorder prepared the mind for the anxieties of the Beyond. The ground was covered with rotting leaves; immense mauve mushrooms surged from the humus and opened like parasols over our heads. Ivy twined around the trunks and the foliage like shadowy snakes. A cuckoo sang its plaintive litany note by note, seeming farther off as we advanced. I noticed the trees were covered with fruit, unlike those in the fields; their little apples were amaranthine or golden yellow in color. I shook a branch, but nothing fell. The low-hanging orbs were well within my grasp, but my fingers lacked the strength to detach them. Growing more and more curious, I yanked a fruit-laden bough and tried to bite, but the apples were iron and nearly broke my teeth. Brindon was anything but reassured by my experience and advised me to keep to simple observation.

"There's no telling where an outrageous appetite will lead," he said.

He had a gift for trivializing any situation.

"Further than frugality, in any case."

"Pardon?"

Once again, I had said nothing. The voice was the same, only closer. I turned my head in every direction.

"What did you say?"

"Brindon, I'm not hallucinating; someone spoke, someone's watching us."

"You should rest for a moment. Hunger is inflaming your imagination and you can't even control your voice anymore . . ."

"Look out, Brindon!"

I scarcely had time to tear him from where he stood: A shoot of ivy detached from a tree and reached out like an arm to ensnare him.

"You scared the living daylights out of me! What's wrong with you?"

"Didn't you see it?"

"What?"

"That ivy."

"So?"

"It was about to strangle you."

The ivy was motionless, still as any creeper. I could not convince the coachman. He looked at me in terror.

"Let's sit down," he said. "I'm nearly done for."

He's talking to me as if I were a madman, I thought. I'll try humor. But nothing amusing came to mind and Brindon just stared at me.

"You must be right. I'm imagining things. Why don't we take a rest?"

I nestled into the thick carpet of leaves and soon fell asleep. When I awoke, Brindon had disappeared. I called and called, I searched every thicket, to no avail. Then I concluded he'd gone back to the carriage and tried to find my way there as well, but I struck out in the wrong direction. I was suddenly panicked and my imagination blazed up again. All the ivy seemed ready to strangle me, the slightest rustle warned of an approaching assassin. Night was falling. The apples in the foliage took on the glitter of gems and were soon incandescent. The big mauve mushrooms were curved to the ground, in the position of sleep. I wove my way forward, intent on avoiding the vegetation, as in those dreams where our slightest inattention can deliver us over to our enemy.

"Brindon!"

There he was, ten yards ahead, frozen at the foot of a tree.

"Brindon, I've been looking for you, you scared the living daylights out of me!"

I moved toward him, his face was pale, his eyes unmoving, his arms stiff against his sides.

"My word, you look like a soldier at attention!"

I gave him a friendly pat on the cheek. It was marble. Shoulders, arms, and chest—all marble. Brindon! A pillar of rock. What I took for staring eyes were agates set in limestone, and the blotch on his cheek, a vein in the marble; only the mustache had the pliancy of life, but it was in fact gray lichen.

I was utterly petrified.

"To see things up close is to be overcome by their distance."

It was the voice, this time in my ear.

"Who are you?"

"Emptiness."

"What do you want from me?"

"Nothing."

"Where's my friend?"

Brindon taps me on the shoulder:

"Shall we?"

"Brindon, Brindon! Where were you? And what's that, over there?"

"What?"

"That stone Brindon, that thing . . ."

"It's nothing, let's go. I've found a path that should bring us back to our starting point. Follow me."

The night is very dark; the light from the apples falls short of the ground and we have to grope our way forward. The vegetation seems thicker, its masses of brambles and vines hinder our progress, the ground is slick, the air moist.

"These autumn nights are unpleasant," says Brindon.

We trip over a pile of rocks. I'm startled; my earlier vision hasn't left my mind. Brindon reassures me. We go around the obstacle.

"Perhaps it's a tumulus," I say.

"We seem to be heading deeper into the forest."

GENEALOGY OF GRAAL FLIBUSTE (CONTINUED)

Dodo, daughter of Jandou and the Ossifrage, bore Palmiped several sons: the Impediments, the Sluts, and the Doles.

The Impediments are wicked beings who roam the mountains and at times settle in overpopulated cities. It is wise to leave food outside your door for them at night; otherwise they break down the door and then, and then . . .

The Sluts, nicknamed the Marionettes, keep to the strawberry fields by preference. They are said to be utterly devoid of intelligence; Phutus, however, relates that a Marionette used a stinkbug to seduce the prettiest peasant girl in Novocordie as she went about her fruit-picking one day. A parallel might be drawn with the tale of Pantala-the-Vicious, reputed by other sources to make love to insects.

Finally, the Doles are ink collectors. They dry inkpots without caps.

Sweet Cha-Cha bore an Impediment named Agactise three sons who were christened the Saints; these characters are not gods, strictly speaking, as they are not immortal. But they are reborn after each death, taking on a different form while keeping their respective attributions; this explains the variety of grigris employed for a given purpose. Din protects against sleeping too deeply; Dan against kidney troubles; Don against bad news in the mailbox. In Dualie we saw mailboxes unlike those in Chanchèze or anywhere else; they were constellated with glass beads, tracery, feathers, and little bronze and copper figurines.

Dan begat Icosohedron whose twenty faces symbolize the twenty perfections one must attain to be considered just. How to catalogue them is often contested by religious historians; some include *sirony*, a virtue midway between silence and mockery that others deliberately reject in favor of *eleglyc*, a mixture of elegance and sweetness. We shall not list these virtues here, subject as they are to controversy.

Icosohedron had twenty daughters, one from each of her faces, known as the Intimate Horrors. They wreak havoc in the subconscious.

Din begat Flutin, who is the dream of love. He is depicted wafting away from a ladder pointed at the sky. He took the natural spring named Song for his wife; she gave him so many daughters and so many sons that the people of this land are commonly heard to say: "It's raining springs and flutes." The story of Song and Flutin is told most admirably by S. Blancasz in his work entitled *Dreaming in Hemiplegics and Cretin-Malthusians*; we could perhaps criticize the work's technical nature, not without a certain anti-poetic effect.

Gladamante, one of Song's daughters, married the poppy Wyly; he carried her off to his kingdom of dwarves. It is said that the poppy's subjects, upon seeing their queen, were so frightened by her size that they disappeared into the forests, where they continue to wander. The primitive populations in the Northwest consider anthills to be the work of these dwarves and condemn anyone who destroys them to death.

Fortyche begat Prak, the sail-less boat. He drifts between heaven and earth, a ferrier of souls whose task it is to reduce the glut of neurasthenics congesting the earth; he is attributed with the power of driving the afflicted to suicide.

Prak begat Flop.
Flop begat Abic.
Abic begat Coucough.
Coucough begat Noodle.
Noodle begat Vertigo.
Vertigo begat Mange.
Mange begat Souiss.
Souiss begat Oop.
Oop begat Fastille-Sebiprim.

Fastille-Sebiprim begat Thornz.

Thornz begat Luquet.

Luquet begat Pamimeter.

Pamimeter begat Nutston.

Nutston begat Affaful.

Affaful begat Boot-Boot.

Boot-Boot begat Lapa.

Lapa begat Yumsk.

Yumsk begat Far.

Far begat Pawt.

Pawt begat Pawt-Pawt.

Pawt-Pawt begat Cornette.

Cornette begat Vallee-Nozay.

Vallee-Nozay begat Torte.

Torte begat Tart.

Tart begat Sweet Preserves.

PHILOSOPHICAL DIALOGUE

"What you're saying is so trite."

"My dear man, I'm not saying anything, I'm relating. Trite? You surprise me. What's coarse is never laughable; I, for one, find it sad. You insist on judging when only your attention is required, and you know it. I wish you wouldn't disappoint me this way."

"I disapprove of bric-a-brac."

"That's why you can't perceive the great beauty of the world."

"If this genealogy is one of its splendors, then I admit I don't understand."

"That's not the point, Brindon. It isn't as if there's a little beauty here, a little ugliness there. What you have, rather, is the whole, the mechanism of the whole. Think big, my dear man, think big."

"What niche will this grandeur of yours find itself next!"

"Grandeur doesn't seek out niches, grandeur soars. We must be like the eagles."

"I suspect you descend now and again from those lofty

heights."

"Once again, Brindon, don't confuse the matter. My weaknesses are mine alone, they're of no consequence, no importance with regard to ..."

"As for me, I like what I can live. Divagations, they're ..."

Oh Brindon, Brindon, to think you're my audience, my only audience! Isn't it pitiful that those we wish to address don't know us, and those with good intentions don't understand us? How very sad ...

We'd left the apple forest two days earlier. Shall I tell the tale of that quagmire and our misadventures there? This is neither the time nor the place, and the memory fills me with a strange mix of sadness and disgust.

THE LOVE QUEST OF THE ENCHANTRESS VAOUA

— I —

The enchantress Vaoua is off on a hunt, off on a hunt for love.

She has donned her sharkskin shoes, her aquamarine dress,

She has combed her blonde tresses, put on her crown of pearls,

But most important are her eyes, she has glazed them with the blood of octopi.

She has fanned her desire with oysters by the three thousand dozen,

And quivering there among the coral reefs, she dives and regains the surface.

But she decides to seek her lovers in the deepest waters, where darkness abets the encounter.

I saw the prophetess Vaoua, her desire was seeping from her every pore,

I was hiding behind a rock and found she was quite to my taste.

But how can a man court a goddess if she feels no desire for him?

And how can a man court love at all when night and deep

damsels distress him?

To be loved, one must provoke, leave one's abode at nightfall

And hang about where drinks are sold.

Or wander through the seaweed, swept by the ebb and flow
that gently sways the shadows.

The prophetess Vaoua knows all the sea's secrets

And were I fish or sand

She'd find me in my hiding place without a moment's pause.

But I, too, am an underwater god

And what I wish to conceal I conceal, my heart is mine
alone,

I resemble men in this, but they know not the danger

Of keeping a secret that neither god nor man can ever know.

The enchantress Vaoua is off on a hunt for love,

She will devastate the small fry, and when she thinks of un-
dressing her victims, she shivers with excitement.

Ah, she says, we'll make a succulent salad,

I'll lure back a dozen and tomorrow we shall see

Who wins out, them or me, adorable runts.

My cuties, my darling fishies, my little flubs,

They have peachy skin, raspberry mouths, pearly bellies,
sugary dongs,

My lemonheads, my caramel drops,

I palp their apricot bottoms as they exhaust themselves on
top of me.

Now they're breathless, perspiring,

I lick up their sweat, it tastes of tears and pleasure.

My tongue moves between their legs

And they're hard again and climbing all over me.

My little mountaineers, my honeyed acrobats, my little
bumblebees, when they whisper in my ear:

"So when do I see you again, you dirty slut?"

I let them talk, I could strangle them

But I need their childish antics.

When I bathe them after my lovemaking,

They wriggle like the fishes they are,

They ask me to rub them dry, to splash them with cologne,

And when they're clean, fragrant, and fresh as mountain daisies,
> We go back to bed and start all over again.
> Oh dear mother, dear old Bath, empress of the waters,
> How I thank you for making me a woman,
> For giving me this bosom, this belly, this nice warm hole
> Where sweet little fleshsticks come and go.
> Around six in the evening I offer them tea and pastries,
> They stuff themselves with babas and éclairs.

The poor boys are beat but their little eyes are beautiful, so
beautiful after we make love
> That I'd like them to die of pleasure.
> Oh the last one, yesterday, how tender and sublime he was
> With his dusky skin and snow-white teeth!

I never grew bored with him, he chased every thought from
my head,
> And he laughed and laughed, which excited me even more.

We ended up on the floorboards gently licking each other's
ears.
> Like two animals weary from a day's work.

— II —

But once the divine Vaoua runs out of money, what will she do
then?
> First of all, she'll be old and ugly,
> And though she may paint her lips red and her lashes green

Though she may slather herself with cod-liver oil to attract
the little fishes,
> Her tricks will be in vain.
> She'll be seen to wander the dark boulevard at night,

Shivering in her tattered mink, her stockings like slack ac-
cordians, her heels worn to the quick,
> She'll end up reading fortunes to earn a few pennies and feel

a man's hands in her own.
> She'll drink by herself in a dirty honky-tonk,
> And since she's immortal, she'll be seen forever and forever-

more.
> People will say "bow-vaow" to her as though she were some

mythological dog.

Poor Vaoua, she'll be miserable!

She'll go to the very bottom of the ocean to sleep, in the remotest corner,

With old women who reek of urine and old men who shit in their drawers.

She'll crawl into a nook all alone with her pot of rotting beans;

She'll nibble on a biscuit that fell from the toilets of a cruise ship,

She'll distantly evoke Jean, Jacques, Philippe, Renaud, Albert, Timoléon,

She won't even have any tears to cry

And will fall asleep with a bitter belch,

Hand upon her stomach.

TOURISM AND TRUISM

We'd come upon some sort of worksite or abandoned city when a local approached us and offered to be our guide:

"This district of useless edifices, unfinished chapels, trompe-l'oeil train stations, roofless casinos, hotel façades, peristyles, clock towers, courtyards, boulevards to nowhere — this district, as I was saying, is reserved for visitors. We spent a lot of money to build it; the materials are top quality and the decorations have been carefully chosen. It's basically our city's museum, even though we've never allowed ourselves a history. We hired a few bogus architects to build this amusement park, so to speak, in the space of a year; we had to keep up with neighboring cities, which have existed for millennia and attract tourists with the prestigious residuum of their successive civilizations. It took us one year to attain three stars in the guidebook — one year of hard, smart work! We use the railroad and cruise ship companies to get our prospectuses out to the public. In our illustrated catalogues, each building in our museum is pictured from the most flattering angle and looks its very best. Anyone would be fooled. What we have is even better than historical monu-

ments, since everything is neat and clean. When visitors are surprised by the excellent condition of these walls, our guides are
under orders to talk about the mysterious restorations under-
taken during the past century, performed with such care that
the Ministry isn't planning any new work for the next three
centuries. We've stuck a few fanciful dates on keystones, lin-
tels, and in hidden corners to make archaeologists gape and history buffs chatter with excitement. Our neighbors have tried
to denounce us using sly counterpropaganda, but nobody believes them; we're invaded by buses of foreigners, workers on
paid vacations, and surprise travel tours. Our hoteliers and inn-
keepers are making a fortune and the mayor offers each visitor a souvenir photograph and a free cocktail. In short, we're
booming. I myself hinted at the last council meeting that another worksite could be created; that way, we'd invest our capital in new construction. The mayor isn't against this, but he says
we need to wait, develop a publicity campaign so far-reaching
that our tourists could actually witness the construction of the
ruins while continuing to believe they're vestiges of the past. I
agreed with this idea, I even applauded it. What delicious perfi-
dy! The mayor surprises us year after year with his intelligence,
his flexibility, his business sense. His project needs to be studied
very closely; we'll put in the hours, set everything up. I'll even
join the guides' association just to relish the visitors' astonish-
ment. We're a resourceful town, with no lack of nerve; we've got
more than one trick up our sleeve! When I talk to the old-tim-
ers around here, I realize that certain traditions don't matter to
us, but mystification, at least, means a lot. It turns out that in
my great grandfather's day—to put things like our neighbors
might—a council member had the idea of situating our city
on a lake and that's how it appeared in the atlases for some fifty
years. We didn't keep it up, because the people who were supposed to take care of the vacationers demanded huge sums for
the energy they spent keeping their clients satisfied by sugges-
tion. But they succeeded. In a sense, you could say our population missed its calling. We like to stay put, we're nationalis-
tic, but we should have emigrated, founded colonies. The world
would have been the better for it. Who can deny the benefi-

cial power of people like us? We impel the masses, whip up enthusiasm, generate business, reinvigorate the blandest clichés,
in short make everybody believe the moon is made of green
cheese, which is what humanity's benefactors are supposed to
do. But now I've detoured into truisms."

CORTEGE

Bizarre animals are crossing a bridge. It's three o'clock or there-
abouts. Beautiful afternoon light. Trees follow the meandering
river and grow slightly bigger as they get further away. Small
white village to the left.

Bizarre animals. Their heads are flat; their legs are jointed
in reverse. You wonder if they're going backward or forward,
which might be a novel experience were it not a bit annoying.
You feel like pushing them one way or the other, because in reality, they're not moving. The pigs, on the other hand, are going forward—what snouts they have!—forward in a dirty line,
drawn as each one is by the dung of the next. Turkey-seals and
lyrebirds are sobbing just like people, but it isn't clear why. Is
this a funeral? An inauguration? There must be a rally somewhere. Meanwhile a malevolent herbivore is strewing marbles in
front of the cortege. They stumble at every step, delighting the
youngsters stationed on the riverbanks. Such a peaceful river!
Not mean or sly, the kind of river everyone would want, entirely liquid, entirely river.

Beside the aforementioned animals, there's the full clique of
monsters with two heads and five legs, but they'd be boring to
describe . . . Here, oh marvel of marvels, is their king. They pull
him on a wagon because of his gout. He wears a pince-nez to
decipher the message he's never known how to read to his people—an old story. Fans are fluttered in front of his face, supposedly to refresh him, but there's malice in this.

Bizarre animals, yes, because they're poor. Wanting for daily
joys, seeking their bread and the small happiness of a coin that
even the humblest ought to be permitted. They are permitted
nothing, so they beg. Gray with dust, they crawl like the bas-

est of creatures, but lack even the serpent's venom. Their heads are lower than their knees and their knees only reach their heels. They dig galleries as they go; through these trenches others follow and flatten them like worms. But they primp and preen and set off once more seeking conquest, in defiance of the enemy. They're heroic. They're rich with unshed tears.

Outlandish, touching cortege, you're as lovely to me as those beautiful stormy afternoons when the rain is long in coming; the heart beats, the breath catches, the mind is set free.

THE FREE MAN

Night was falling. Since morning we'd been trundling through a hilly countryside, pleasant and abounding with wild currants and blackberries. The day had rolled by easily, inducing a mild form of torpor; we had stopped at noon to gather fruit and stretch our legs.

We took up our quarters under a catalpa where we found some blueberries. As we lay on Clotho's cover, I told Brindon this fable before falling asleep:

"Then the king rose and said: 'Release the prisoner.' His henchmen let me go. I was so overcome I couldn't move, then my legs gave way. I'd been imprisoned for a month, awaiting my death sentence. The king's cruelty was known throughout the world; my friends were already in mourning. There was even talk that I'd be boiled alive. This torture, last inflicted during the Middle Ages, was to be brought back in my honor. I grew accustomed to this terrifying idea, or rather tried to push it from my mind through prolonged exercises intended to put myself in a daze, pacing in my cell until exhausted or banging my head against the wall. I had lost much of my strength, I scarcely ate anymore, and little by little a sort of numbness came over me.

"I regained consciousness in an antechamber, as buckets of water were being dumped over my head. The idea of my liberty appeared to me in the form of a face, a real face above me, and I reached out to touch it with my hand. The men around me thought I was asking for assistance; they pulled me by the arm, but I couldn't remain upright. I was taken to the infirmary where I once again lost consciousness for several days. I don't know what kind of treatment I received; I awoke one morning in a bed that was more or less clean, surrounded by other patients. Expecting that I'd die at any moment, they were surprised when I opened my eyes. They questioned me. I could not answer. The face above me no longer had the same features; it was now a replica of my own face. In my lethargic state, I imagined myself as this other being watching myself suffer. I had become this implacable face that could not stand my presence on the bed, and I weakly asked to be exterminated. Someone gave me something to drink. The idea of my liberty had transformed itself into a profound self-hatred. This lasted several days. I regained my strength little by little and my double disappeared; in the days that followed, it was as though I'd come through a fever and was enjoying a well-being beyond words; but alas, convalescence reaches an end, health returns, and here I am today cured and free."

"What are you trying to say?" Brindon asked me.

"No idea, really. But we could talk of more realistic things, if you like."

BLAND TALK

He responded straightaway:

"My grandmother, who was losing her sense of smell, took the desire to please so far as to pretend she only liked bland foods; in the company of others, she adroitly dissimulated, but in her room she ate mustard and caper sandwiches."

"On that note," I said, "I know a vinegar brewer who had 'For discriminating palates since 1789' printed on his labels. Do you think there's an allegorical link with the Revolution? And, by the same token, with the expression 'you catch more flies with honey than with vinegar'?"

"Your vinegar brewer would have to be terribly witty, sir, and I am not certain that profession . . ."

"Don't be led astray. There are witty people everywhere."

"But so many more are oafs! I get infuriated when people explain something that couldn't be clearer or more obvious, then ask: 'Do you see what I mean?'"

"That kind of silliness doesn't upset me. I find you quite aggressive ... one must be compassionate, adopt the common man's tastes, take up his trite opinions ..."

"Hm, hm."

"That's what I've surmised, my dear man. One has experiences, believes them crazy or at least eccentric, yet still reaches conclusions of such banality ... Wisdom. For example, I'm convinced that love is based on sacrifice; a conclusion I'd have gladly foregone, but that's how it is. You see what I mean ..."

"Hm."

"My conclusions du jour all amount to clichés. I assure you this isn't humiliating, on the contrary."

"I've known you to have more bite ..."

"Incisiveness is not an ideal. But the cliché is. In parallel, I would say that worriers are the most selfish of people."

"I don't see the connection."

"I said, in parallel."

"I don't see the parallel."

"Too bad. Yes, worriers. I know someone who agonizes over trivia; he might seem sensitive to an outsider, but to those who know him he's an egomaniac, and can even be a lout. Anxiety over little things is not sensitivity, which is a doorway to the outside, an openness toward others; no, this kind of anxiety is sentimentality, which is the opposite of sensitivity."

"You're splitting hairs. Sensitivity may well be diverted from its object by a serious inner conflict."

"You believe in inner conflicts?"

"What?"

"I don't believe in them. Only surface shocks exist."

"Words, sir, nothing but words."

"What feeds conversations?"

"Ideas."

"What's an idea?"

"It's when a person has something to say."

"Hm . . . I would add, incidentally, that only the truth deserves our sanction. The expression 'speak the truth' used to call to mind the image of an uncouth man with a rough handshake, someone who's always right, which is why the words upstanding, frank, and loyal used to fill me with the utmost horror. Probably some brute said to possess these qualities had barred the serene images they ought to have evoked from my mind; truth ended up unrecognizable, masked by brutality. Such a stupid confusion, isn't it? Truth is so nuanced, so subtle, so diverse; to side with truth is to attempt the most perilous acrobatics, the most . . ."

"Hm."

"This isn't casuistry, my dear man. I'm saying that to disguise one's thinking is to risk becoming a brute. The proposition is reversed."

LADY NATURE

The following day I awoke before Brindon. Our catalpa was in full flower. Overnight, the delicate clusters had blossomed, snow in the sun of morning. I got up and, to reinforce our recently formed habits, I set out in search of game. I followed the course of a stream, brushing past the snowbells and lesser celandine along its banks. What kindness in this April morning! Fresh memories came back to me. Distant childhood, we dip into your treasures at the slightest hint of well-being, as if all sensual delights released some secret spring and made you surge up once again.

The countryside resembled a garden in which rare shrubs alternated with rock sculptures, hedges, ponds ablaze with color, natural terraces, and labyrinths of overarching branches. I stepped into one of these mazes, surprised that this sophisticated construction was the work of nature; man has done nothing, I thought, that nature didn't do before him, with less rigor perhaps, but with so much generous fantasy! Ah, the generosity of nature is grand, and we diminish it in ourselves with

arbitrary choices, with laws, whereas allowing our passions to
guide us would do much more to further our knowledge of the
world. With these words, I stumbled on a root and fell headfirst into a holly bush; had nature planned this affront? The
great master of ceremonies, chance, had favored me with its
solicitude. I climbed out of my holly bush. In a corner of the
labyrinth, I discovered a litter of puppies being fed by a wild
goose. Then a brood of nightingales holding up their beaks to a
panther. Then a swarm of mosquitoes under the care of a hen.
My surprise was complete when I saw the trompe-l'oeil of a
termites' nest masking a reserve of smoked ham and haddock.
Ah, I thought, our ration will be easily won; what surprises our
good Mother has in store for us! But then someone grabbed
me by the back of the neck and shoved me into an oubliette.
Once accustomed to the darkness, I was able to make out a female dog, a nightingale, and a mosquito. "Vengeance!" cried a
voice, probably that of the native who had assailed me. I looked
through the keyhole and saw a terrifying mask. "Our torturer,"
said the dog. I understood that a drama was unfolding in which
the victims were these innocent mothers. "Is it natural for us
to be deprived of our young?" asked the nightingale. "Natural, natural . . ." I stammered, "no, it's not natural. I mean . . ."
"You mean?" "There are things in nature, Madame . . ." "You
clearly have no wife or family, Monsieur. We know nature better than you do." And she fell to lamenting. "I'm not siding
with nature against you," I said. "Hear me out . . ." "Your words
are absurd," said the mosquito acridly. "How can you conceive
of being for or against anyone in this situation? We are mothers
naturally devastated by an injustice of nature." I acknowledged
the wisdom of this insect who always knows where to bite. The
problem was insoluble. What would become of me? I was neither a mother nor deprived of my offspring. Was I going to be
assigned with an orphan brood to feed, like goose, panther, and
hen? I was imagining myself dumbly suckling millipedes or ant-
eaters when the jailer knocked at the door. He came in.

"You, out," he said to me.

"May I ask for your clemency on behalf of these three individuals?"

"Don't worry about them, they're only getting their due. As denatured mothers, that is."

"Denatured? How so?"

"That's none of your affair. Follow me."

I understood I was going to be judged. He led me to a bust of lard installed under a dome of greenery. I was to undergo a kind of judgment by God. It was explained to me that if my fire-reddened finger left a hole in the bust, my fate would be sealed. I was witness to all the preparations, then to the amputation of my finger, then to the test. What anguish! But I came out victorious. They threw me from the labyrinth without so much as a farewell.

It was snowing. The season had regressed; the garden was wintery under its white mantle. I did not like this unnatural phenomenon and hid my head under a sheet.

THE ORGANIST

But at the far end of a black chapel, at the top of a dungeon hemmed in by crows, three hundred floors above the moat, for the castle is a city, in the gusty winds of the heights, grit of stone and scorch of fire, with an unassailable joy in his heart, the old organist, as twisted as a mandrake, was playing for God alone a phrase seven thousand times seven times repeated, hammered out, cut, dissected, melted down, and started over again, as if in hazarding forth from his brain it would—through the torture he inflicted on himself to restate it—return to its original nothingness for having remained inaudible and carry the musician into the hiccup of its ultimate variation; thus died the melody—childhood, maturity, old age—beaten out to the rhythm of the blood, denying the rhythm of the hour, having become perception, bone, flesh, forgetful of itself as he is of his years, this father of voiceless children, his vigor sacrificed to perfecting the phrase, and all the possible harmonics, which no cantor, in the proscribed morning hours of the chapel, could ever again make known to a human ear.

TITI

Brindon, who'd awakened a few minutes earlier, was waiting for me under the catalpa. When he saw me arrive without provender, he stifled a fit of temper; I enjoyed his annoyance then took the two nosey-snoops from my pocket that I'd gathered on my way back. His appetite being what it is, he clapped his hands: "Hurry, hurry, into the pot," he said.

Nosey-snoops are a variety of ox tongue, half-plant, half-invertebrate. They crawl like slugs and are reddish in color. Some grow as big as beavers. You can fry them quite nicely with a clove of garlic, or use wild scallions instead. I'd also found a stalk of meos, the juices of which are delectable. Brindon stretched out lazily on his blankets and I was about to slice the nosey-snoops when a young nagar appeared from behind a tamarack and began to prance about in front of us. I danced a little minuet with this delicious plantigrade creature, making Brindon forget his hunger. Then the father nagar appeared and immediately reassured us of his good intentions; he'd come out of curiosity and not as an enemy. Unfamiliar with this animal's tastes, I could think of nothing to offer him; then he noticed the stalk of meos I'd left near the fire. He gazed at it so longingly I was happy to give it to him; Brindon looked on begrudgingly as he wolfed it down. In thanks, the nagar offered us his son, since his female was expecting again. "Family is well and good," he said, "but plenty is too much." We laughed at his pleasantry. The nagaron was enchanted to find himself in our hands and gleefully offered to take over the cooking. I politely protested, unaware that nagars are the best cooks in the world.

We chatted for a moment about the little nothings of the forest, seduction among the nagars, their society and government. They seemed well regulated by their constitution and showed no interest in changing it; the very thought of altering their customs seemed ridiculous to our host. He was surprised at our taste for risk—we'd briefly told him the aim of our voyage—and he invited us to stay with him and rest awhile. "What works itself up can wind itself down," he said. He could not have been more amiable. Then he took his leave, instructing

his son to make himself useful at every opportunity. We were
to meet him the following day around lunchtime at his wife's
home.

I let Titi (that was the child's name) prepare the meal at
his insistence and went back to where I'd found the meos to
gather more. When I returned, I found the table laid, Brindon
quite impatient, and Titi flushed with emotion; he was afraid
we might not like how he'd seasoned the nosey-snoops. But we
loved them. Brindon belched loudly, much to the delight of
Titi who nearly choked trying to imitate him. Ah, what simple pleasures we've adopted, and I'll never be able to recall these
hours of noisy digestion without a touch of nostalgia!

After lunch, the nagaron busied himself by carving reeds
into little flutes and charmed us with his playing. His expressions were droll; he would throw back his head in a simulation
of ecstasy, eyes half-closed. He had a vast knowledge of music;
he told us he'd learned from someone we'd have the surprise of
meeting the following day. Titi played for us sylvan airs full of
melancholy, alpine airs full of gaiety, maritime airs full of salt.
I can but transcribe the lyrics he improvised for one of them:

> "We the nagars, who will build us boats?
> We have our bees to feed,
> And the house of the boss to clean,
> He treats us like his friends;
> Will we leave him here to set sail?"

Quite exquisite, I'd say. The nagaron improvised many more,
ending with a lullaby full of languor that had its effect on Brindon; he was sleeping when Titi put down his flutes and nestled against him with animal grace. All three of us took a nap;
it must have been about four o'clock. At six, I was awakened by
a cuckoo and beheld the most delicious of spectacles: Brindon's
plumed hat had slipped over Titi's head and the young nagar,
looking like a budding musketeer, his arms around the coachman's neck, smiled at the angels of his dreams.

The evening promised to be brisk, so I awoke my sleep-
ers. We lit a fire of twigs and deliberated over dinner preparations. Titi, who knew his native forest by heart, told me of a

place where one could capture a type of game I'd never heard of, which he could only describe with the imprecision of children his age. A sort of aquatic hare, from what I could surmise, whose succulent fat was used to prepare any number of pastries. We decided to leave Brindon the task of gathering and peeling vegetables at his leisure, and set off, Titi and I, with the traps we'd made from willow, for the areas inhabited by our hare.

THE SLUDGE HARES

We approached the edges of a vast swamp. Titi advised me to keep quiet, then set about adroitly tying his knots and finding the most suitable locations. Next he asked that I light a cigarette; the sludge hare has a penchant for smoke, he told me. A few minutes went by as I feverishly inhaled my Gauloise and Titi kept watch for any movement in the reeds.

"I see one," he said under his breath.

"Where?"

"Over there."

"I don't see anything."

"There, in the sludge," he whispered.

A vaguely circular movement could be seen rippling through the mud, then something pointed appeared . . .

"That's its ear," said Titi. "Shh. Keep smoking."

I lit a second cigarette. The ear emerged completely, then the head. It resembled the head of a fennel-eating doll, detached and worn as a mask during traditional mid-Lent festivities. I waited for the second ear, but there was only one. Next the front legs came into view. The hare sniffed and turned toward us. Titi pressed himself against me. Shh, shh. With great exertion, the animal freed its hind quarters and dragged its way to a dry place where it started to lick itself clean.

"We have to let it eat a lot of sludge," murmured Titi. "That's what makes it taste good."

The hare frequently interrupted its work to relish the smoke pushed downward by the heavy air. Once it had finished its toilette, it moved in our direction, advancing cautiously as if to avoid dirtying its paws. I could feel Titi's heart pounding.

Would his trap do the trick? The hare approached, visibly attracted by the smell of tobacco. Caught in the gin, it yelped in pain. "A female!" said the nagaron. "We're in luck, the meat is juicier, and maybe she has gelatinous babies for the bouillon." He hoped that the doe was pregnant. We approached the animal, which the willow had very nearly strangled. Titi finished her off with his pocketknife. I was about to detach our prey when my companion grabbed my arm.

"Don't move—here comes the male! Keep smoking."

The senses of hunters are infinitely more developed than our own; like their sense of smell, their vision may become extraordinarily keen. Titi pointed to where he thought the male would emerge. Indeed, the sludge moved, then out came the ear, then the entire animal. We didn't have any nooses left. Titi told me to wait until the buck had gorged itself on sludge from his grooming. Then Titi undid his belt, which was wrapped three or four times around his waist, and fashioned a lasso, catching the hare so rapidly I barely had time to see his maneuver. "Two down!" he cried joyously.

Having rinsed our hares in the stream, we took them back to the camp. Brindon looked askance when he saw them; I would have done the same. These creatures are rather repulsive, as much because of their dingy gray color and misshapen bodies as because of the odor they give off. But Titi assured us we would never taste a more delicate meat. "And this bouillon, my dear friends, I know you'll love it." My mouth wasn't exactly watering, knowing as I did what the said bouillon would consist of; the doe was in fact pregnant. We turned ourselves over to the culinary talents of our friend, however, and waited for the meal while confabulating, Brindon and I, as if we'd been familiars for years.

The next day, we were so enjoying the company of our nagaron that we decided against visiting his parents and took another French leave, packing our bags and clearing out. Clotho was livelier than ever and Brindon had taken care to grease the axles of the carriage. We would use the fat of the hares for this purpose, as Titi had lacked flour for the cakes. Poor Titi! We were to pay dearly for our friendly feelings toward him and the ingratitude we showed his parents. A few hours after we left, he fell ill; we stopped on the side of the road and watched helplessly as an unforgiving disease ran its lightening course: nagaritis. He died in our arms. We left him to the carrion-eaters and set out once more, filled with bitterness. But our experience of a companion, however brief, had left us inclined to appreciate the company of others; unsociable though Brindon and I were, being each other's only confidant was growing dull. So it is that the possessiveness one feels for another loses its edge, as if the refusal to share another's company with anyone else contains the seeds of an inevitable break. But this image exceeds the bounds of my relationship with Brindon, devoid of any reciprocal passion.

THE HOSTESS

We came to a peninsula planted with camphor trees. Little enclosures indicated the presence of natives. Continuing on for nearly half a day, we finally saw a cluster of buildings rising above the foliage.

"Is it prudent to venture into the village with the carriage?" I asked Brindon.

"We'd perhaps do well to unhitch here and make a reconnaissance on foot."

We unhitched. For the first time, Clotho was exhausted; he lay on the grass in a near-faint. It was probably the lack of oats. Or some vague apprehension? It seemed fitting to arm myself with the old percussion rifle that the coachman kept in the carriage trunk; not that I knew how to shoot, but carrying a gun would give me confidence. The coachman watched me with a smile.

"We're looking very prudent."

"You know my taste for humor, dear man."

We tied Clotho to a camphor tree, blocked the wheels of the carriage with a chain, and headed for the village. Our precautions made me uneasy, as if preparing for an incident would inevitably provoke it. And yet nature seemed so welcoming, so beautiful!

We walked for about a league; then some distance before the

hamlet, we took detour. Concealed by a slight incline, we were able to approach the first houses from behind, on the forest side. I could now understand the role of the forest in the history of strategy: What could be more favorable to a captain's stratagems than the ruses of nature herself? Shadows, shrouds of trees, entangled paths — any number of obstacles that slow the enemy yet abet those who have learned to use them. We thereby arrived one hundred yards or so from the last houses and, hidden behind a cluster of trees, we observed.

A ghastly creature came out of a stable; it was carrying a bucket that apparently contained milk. The creature put the bucket down in the middle of the courtyard and scratched. Its head formed a single unit with its body, which was difficult to distinguish as male or female. It had no shoulders, and its ears seemed attached to its biceps. Shaggy locks fell every which way, masking half its face, falling down around its buttocks, and getting stuck as the shapeless creature moved. I was still overcoming my stupor, as was Brindon, when the thing picked up its bucket and headed to the dung heap to empty it; we could tell by liquid's color that it was urine. The creature wavered an instant, seemed to look in our direction, and then went inside the house. Brindon asked whether I was planning on getting acquainted with these animals. I replied in the affirmative, since there was at least a fifty percent chance they were hospitable. Who's to say they didn't cook with butter? Who's to say they didn't sleep in beds? "Who's to say they aren't divine in bed?" added Brindon lightly. "I could care less about that," I retorted. "But a bed, that's my aspiration of the moment. I'm weary of camping."

We stepped out of our hiding place and made our way toward the door where the monster had disappeared. We were none too reassured; I held fast to the rifle and Brindon to a cudgel he was concealing under under his peacoat. We reached the house and tried to look through the window, but a sackcloth obscured our view. Not daring to lift it, I decided to knock on the door. No answer. I knocked louder. Still no answer.

"Maybe the thing is deaf," Brindon said to me. "Let's open

the door a little."

We opened the door a little. The creature was stretched out on the floor tiles, apparently asleep. Should we wake it? I asked Brindon with a look; he seemed undecided. I coughed. The creature moved its feet. I coughed again. The creature opened its eyes, which were gray and edged with pink; upon seeing us, it responded with wild terror, folding its knees against its chin and encircling them with both arms, still lying on its back. At this point we realized it was female. To mollify her, I smiled and made some round gesture or other with my arms, without moving toward her. She seemed less afraid. It then occurred to me to sit on the floor—Brindon sat as well—to persuade her our intentions were peaceful. This worked. She sat on her haunches and stared at us, the terrified expression having left her face.

"Do you understand me?" I ventured.

She nodded.

"Do you live here alone?"

"Yes."

"And . . . does the village have many inhabitants?"

"Yes."

She didn't seem inclined to chat. I then asked if she could put us up for the night. She jumped to her feet so fast she nearly startled us to death. Then she rushed to the pantry, took out some victuals, laid the table, lit the fire—in short made haste like the most able of housewives. Strange, strange creature!

We proceeded to eat the meal she'd prepared, consisting of boiled green acorns and camphor sausages; our hunger made the entire thing seem delectable. Conversation after dinner was sparse and the evening came to an early close. Our hostess had practically refused to speak; was this stupidity, or rather consideration? In any case, it wasn't hostility. She offered us the big bed in her boudoir and went up to the second floor like a well-mannered person. I fell asleep immediately, as did Brindon. But I suspect he spent part of the night upstairs; when I awoke around four in the morning, he was not beside me. I fell asleep again and when I awoke at noon, he was sweeping the floor and whistling. He refrained from any confidences.

THE CAMPHORPHAGES

We lunched with our hostess. This time, I was not pleased to see the camphor soup arrive. The salad tasted strongly of camphor as well, like the liqueur that was supposed to be our digestif. Afterward, Brindon and I visited the village. The news of our arrival had created quite a stir; the poor villagers were hanging around their doorsteps. All of them had the same ill-made body as our hostess, but their courtesy was admirable; they all prostrated themselves humbly as we passed. We entered some of the houses. All of them were alike and all of them harbored the same detestable odor. These people generally have five or six children, blob-like before puberty, at which point they take shape, so to speak. I patted a few of them politely, but the feel of their greasy hair and clammy skin was more than I could stand. The children are crammed into the kitchens and courtyards; they hardly move. Their parents work in the camphor fields and that's the lot of it; no community pastimes, no village festivities, no ceremonies ever, not a one. Hence their hangdog expression, I thought, softening toward them. They have neither laws nor councils, governing themselves naturally. There's a school that supposedly teaches the rudiments of language to the youth when they leave the nest, but they are just awakening to their senses at that point and end up fornicating with each other rather than developing their minds. Since their mothers are loath to speak to them and their schooling is unfruitful, the young Camphorphages learn to express themselves only belatedly. Speech is not esteemed by the population.

Near the end of our visit, we were approached by a man less deformed than his kinfolk; his expression was also more alert. He invited us in for refreshments. "Yet another round of camphor," I murmured to Brindon. But to our surprise and satisfaction the man poured us a variety of anisette not unlike our traditional Pernod. I was unable to mask a sigh of relief. "Terrible, all this camphor, isn't it?" remarked the man.

"A question of habit, I imagine," replied Brindon courteously.

"I, for one, have never gotten used to it," continued our host. "It so happened that I was passing through these parts, a tourist like yourselves, some twenty years ago. I was cornered by one of the female natives who then married me. Living with my wife — she died last year — I ended up looking like a Camphorphage, but, as I said, I've never adopted their tastes. Incidentally, these people are very easy to live with. I appreciate their indifference, their self-effacement; they know nothing of jealousy and gossip."

At his first words, I elbowed Brindon, who knew immediately what I was hinting at and blushed like a schoolboy. I couldn't help but laugh as I thought of his adventure the previous night and the risk he ran of sharing our host's fate. The man offered to put us up for the rest of our stay; I was about to accept, then reconsidered, out of respect for Brindon, who said not a word. Ah the bed, I thought, such enslavement! What happened next proved me right.

LIMP FISH

Leaving the anisette man, we took a walk through the environs of the town before dinner, following a path lined with poor man's asparagus. I told my coachman we should gather a few handfuls and prevail on our hostess to prepare it; I was a bit apprehensive about our evening gruel. Brindon thought we might offend the lady. I did not reply.

The path led us to a little pond pullulating with fish; we could see them jumping out of the water and snatching at flies. Why not catch a few, I thought; we'll find some way to fry them. I fashioned a makeshift pole using rushes and string I found lying about, with a bent hatpin for a hook and a sludgey worm for bait. Brindon wandered off alone, a dreamy look in his eye. I threw myself into my improvised sport and caught so many fish that the bank was soon covered with them. The moment they left the water they died, without the slightest twitch, and went limp. I soon tired of such easy prey and tossed my tackle, pole and all, into the pond. Then I tried to pull Brindon from his reveries so we could gather up my loot. But this proved impossible. The first fish I'd caught were already decomposing into gelatin, or rather into a goop that stuck to our fingers. A quarter of an hour later, nothing remained on the bank except the thinnest of shiny films.

"An image of our destiny," I said, attempting to bring the matter to some kind of conclusion.

"Easy enough for you to say," grumbled the coachman.

What did he mean? You must have something else on your mind, Brindon . . .

"We'd better go if we want to get back before nightfall."

Very well. We returned to the path and silently made our way to the village, then the house. Our hostess had prettied herself up with a red kerchief for her head and a sort of peignoir rolled around her hips. She had smoothed her hair into straight, flat locks; a big wooden bracelet adorned her wrist and strings of camphor beads hung about her ankles. Surreptitiously observing Brindon, I saw his eyes flash. We sat down to our meal but I couldn't eat a single bite. My commensals, on the other hand, glutted themselves. Dessert was served. Then all at once our hostess informed me:

"Now I'm going to sleep with him, you go sleep upstairs."

Brindon was cowardly enough to lower his head without a word. I would have liked to tell him that I found all this natural enough but hoped it wouldn't last; we had better things to do than remain caught in this siren's nets. But could I be misjudging her intentions?

I spent the night lost in thoughts as futile as they were exhausting.

A PREMEDITATED CRIME

Two months. This disgusting affair lasted two months! I could stand it no longer, I was up to my nose in Camphorphages, as they say. I'd taken up residence with the anisette man, finding the debasement of my coachman intolerable. Something had to be done to tear Brindon away from this creature. Reasoning with him was pointless; he dismissed my objections as sanctimonious blather. I made up my mind to take drastic measures. To kill, to kill. One can't imagine how comfortable this idea becomes over time, or how natural its execution. I simply cut off her head as she slept, one afternoon when Brindon was away. I ran the risk that Brindon might kill me in turn, but I accepted this risk. How to describe my shock when, on the lookout for the coachman, I saw him freeze in front of the cadaver, his eyes suddenly ferocious; then he kicked and trampled his mistress with shouts of hatred and joy. I thought he'd gone mad. When I emerged from my hiding place, Brindon threw himself into my arms. We spoke at length. He'd been under a spell, the woman had used magical powers. If only I'd thought sooner to rid the world of her presence! Brindon's hatred extended to all the Camphorphages, even though they probably didn't deserve this. In less than an hour, we'd left the village.

THE MOUNTAIN

. . . But still we hesitated. The road on the right wound up a high mountain; the road on the left dropped into a wooded valley abloom with jollz. I don't know what decided me in favor of the mountain; Brindon left the matter in my hands and we set out for the summits. The morning was beautiful and the heat unobtrusive, but the sharp incline slowed our progress considerably. I was not displeased with my decision, the landscape would change and the air would be invigorating; the low altitudes left us feeble and dispirited. Burbling springs, dry and fragrant vegetation, sweeping views of the plain—all these alpine sensations would inspire our bodies and refresh our souls. Brindon was as happy as if he'd awakened from a bad dream; he acquiesced to my every whim. As for Clotho, it wasn't long before we relieved him of our weight so that an agreeable hike could be had by all.

A clump of rhododendron caught my eye. It seemed to be moving. I pointed this out to the coachman who, more through kindness than conviction, agreed with me. He brought Clotho to a halt and we observed that the clump was indeed climbing the slope. I approached the plant, which, on closer examination, turned out to be a most curious beast, a sort of flowering porcupine. I couldn't distinguish the head from the rest of the body and stared with repugnance for a moment; when I finally stretched out my hand toward the corollas, they immediately invaginated like the tentacles of an actinia. I could then see how they were arranged on the animal's carapace, which I turned over. Its belly was a downy gray, with eighteen legs and three eyes dotting the abdomen here and there. From an orifice, either mouth or anus, the animal sprayed me with an exquisitely scented jet of bluish nectar. It occurred to me to take the little flask I always carry in my pocket and fill it with the liquid, which I did by pressing the animal's belly. It expired soon afterward; all of its flowers had wilted. I named this creature the rhodopork and its fragrance blue ambrosia.

KING GNAR

We came upon a chatty colporteur who traveled with us for a spell. He told us about the routes he took through the area and all sorts of regional stories. That of King Gnar stands apart:

"In the mountain, my good sirs, there is a cavern. A deep, branching cavern with several diverticula leading to external openings, each far from the others, as in a gigantic burrow. This cavern is inhabited; there lives King Gnar with his household. The king is a powerful lord. His household includes his wife, Queen Tonfe, six children including three boys and three girls, his old mother, Pirogue, his uncle Chiste, and twenty or so servants selected from the populations on the plain and in the surrounding valleys. The king worships Graal Flibuste and every morning climbs Mount Rot to recite the divine office. Three servants accompany him, carrying three lambs and a jug of kerosene; at the summit the king kneels down to pray while the servants slit the lambs' throats and quickly burn the animals on pyres built the day before. The king gives thanks to the god for making him what he is, gazes across the arc of his lands, and makes his way back to the cavern. His daughters have prepared a meal; no sooner does their father return than they diligently serve him. The fresh air has whetted the king's appetite;

his spirits are high and while eating he jests with his daughters:

"'When will we marry you off, young ladies? When? Not a suitor in sight for any of you, your station in life places you above everyone else.'

"'With all due respect, Father, don't forget that we are women first and foremost, that's our true station,' says Marie.

"'And don't forget that our mother was a wench in a big restaurant; she had no other station than the love you felt for her,' says Solange.

"'Moreover, sir,' says the youngest daughter, 'our brothers are going to leave us; doesn't your station in life require three sons-in-law? Who will take care of the livestock, and the personnel, and the buildings?'

"The king smiles. His counselor and friend is a serpent known as the Ox. He is coiled under Gnar's chair and when he hears his master fold his napkin, he slides his head between the arm of the chair and the royal thigh. The king lets him nibble the ham rind on the edge of his plate, then gets up, casually carrying his counselor on his shoulder. They go off to work.

"Queen Tonfe awakens; she calls for her daughters who embrace her and help her plan out the day. As for the three brothers, they've left to hunt and won't return before noon. The usual staff are to be found in the kitchens, the stables, the fields.

"What does King Gnar attend to in his office? Neither politics nor economics. The Ox divulges the great secrets of metaphysics to him and cultivates his gift for clairvoyance. The Ox was adopted by his master during a voyage that the then-prince made to the far reaches of the Orient; the Ox was a magician's snake, a serpent savant. When Gnar entered the magician's hut, the first thing he saw was the Ox. He couldn't take his eyes off him for the entire consultation. The magician gave his serpent to Gnar; for he realized that theirs was a love at first sight, which is sacred. Gnar took the serpent with him and his joy was so profound that he couldn't bear to leave the land of his love. He stayed for several years on the banks of the Santiar River with the Ox, who taught him astrology and other occult sciences. Neither would have left this haven had a telegram not arrived for Gnar

announcing the death of his father; the son's obligation was
to return home for the succession. They returned. Gnar had
a little trouble convincing his mother to accept the Ox; then
Pirogue grew so preoccupied with the young king's wedding
that she forgot everything else. When Queen Tonfe arrived, she
had the finesse not to ask her spouse to explain his feelings for
the animal, and their life together was most happy and calm."

THE CHERRY TREE OF THE DEAD

We arrived that evening in a little hamlet situated along a torrent. An ancient inn welcomed us for the night. With our colporteur's stories, the hours slipped by unnoticed. The room we
sat in was softly lit and smelled of resin; we sipped a juniper liqueur of the highest quality.

"As for this village," the colporteur went on, "I knew it well
before the catastrophe swept everything away, so to speak; the
mountainside it was built on collapsed, leaving nothing but
these scattered houses. There used to be terraces, an alpine garden, a village hall, a church, and the most adorable cemetery I
ever saw. One summer evening, wandering about dreamily, I
came to the cemetery. In the middle of it was a big cherry tree,
all covered with cherries.

"The countryside was bathed in moonlight, the air was
warm, I could hear the rushing torrent and the song of the
nightingale. At the time, I was in love with a girl in a village
not far from here; my thoughts drifted to my sweetheart. The
splendid cherry tree held out its fruit, which I ate by the hundreds in one of those fits of voracity typical of my age. I fell
asleep under the tree and awoke when it was barely light. That's
when I saw that the cherries were the eyes of the dead. Their
bloody eyes, hanging from the stems."

Comical as he'd been during the day, our storyteller was
becoming macabre. I suggested we retire to spare the three of
us nightmares. The innkeeper led the way to our room where
three beds awaited us. Brindon had no sooner collapsed on his
than he was fast asleep. The colporteur and I continued to con-
fabulate, waiting for sleep to overtake us.

"Have you ever been to the other side of the mountain?" I asked him.

"No, sir, I've never been further than Impediment Pass. But my father used to visit the other side, he was a colporteur like me. He met my mother here, then brought her to the province I was born in. When my father died I came here with my mother, who wanted to return to her mountains to live out her remaining days. She died three years ago, at my Aunt Agatha's place. My aunt is still alive; she lives with Martha along with Louis and Julien, my first cousins. Louis is Françoise's widower and Julien married Martha . . ."

It was time I bid our companion goodnight.

THE SERPENT

The serpent coils himself, the familiar serpent, in tenebrous thoughts, well known to princes and brigands, sweetening the heart that warms him; he comes from faraway lands where righteous men are disdained, he eats at the enemy's table. Fair prince with your confidant, your words are interpreted against you. The serpent obtained three crowns he bestowed upon thieves; the king searches the gilded case. Well you may search; your crowns are lost.

"What is hiding in this mountain, fleeing with the torrent and the cascade? A king resides there, the pupil of a serpent, gone to earth in a cavern with numerous outlets. He got wind of my aspiration to reach the summit. This mountain, where the invisible dwells, what is it?"

"This mountain, trite little tourist, this mountain too carelessly selected . . . your power doesn't extend that far. How easy it is to evoke a plain and believe in it, a sky and reside in it, but say what you will of this mountain, it is higher than either plain or sky and dominates both."

"And this king, who is he, and this serpent, are they the products of chance, why a ridiculous king and a stagecraft snake?"

"Because you degrade everything you touch, his guards are commensurate with the prisoner in your fables."

"In this sack," says the mountain, "I have a candied serpent, a serpent good enough to eat, he no longer has any teeth, he no longer has the strength to climb out." "In this head," says the serpent, "I have all the world's cunning and all the world's ploys, every means of casting love into doubt. I climb out of the sack at night, I slither among the drinkers. They drink until they can't see their neighbors, music accompanies them to the edge of the river where the boats are waiting for them, they take their seats and disappear under the willow trees, the waters that lull them make their senses waver, the bottom of the boat falls away, and in their madness each one accuses the others."

ALERT IN THE CAVERN

One morning after breakfast, when Gnar and the Ox had withdrawn to their study, the serpent asked in a syrupy voice:

"Sire, what is an enemy?"

"Someone who wants to wrong us."

"Is it wrong to violate the territory of a neighbor?"

"It's a crime."

"And how do we punish this crime?"

"By arresting and killing the enemy."

"And what if the enemy feigns ignorance of our borders?"

"Inculcation by the guillotine."

The serpent rubs his hands.

"Sire, do you have any enemies?"

"Not that I'm aware of."

"Do you have borders?"

"I do, by Jove!"

"So whoever violates your borders is your enemy?"

"Yes, by George!"

"Well then, Sire, prepare your guillotine."

"What?"

"Your borders were trespassed this morning."

"Good heavens! By whom?"

"Two travelers in a carriage."

"Monsters! Where did they come from?"

"Chanchèze, Sire. And I suspect from even farther away than that."

The king said, "Something must be done," and rang for his top armorer, his general, and his executioner. The relevant personnel were armed, the sentinels put on guard, the guillotine in place. "We're waiting, dear travelers."

The princesses lamented; they're sensitive and know nothing of politics. And they were picturing two tired yet noble travelers, poor yet charming.

"Horrors!" said Solange. "Our father is preparing to kill innocent men. What shall we do?"

"I'm thinking," said Marie, "I'm thinking furiously."

"I daresay you'd be unwise," said the youngest daughter, "to endanger the security of the State. Why this sudden rebellion, by such submissive demoiselles? How vaingloriously you see yourselves! One cannot reinvent who one is."

"One can perfect who one is, dear Sister."

And hatch plots, and lay plans.

"Shall we inform Mother?" Solange asked.

"Perish the thought," said Marie. "That could very well spoil everything."

Whereas the queen had been listening all the while, her ear pressed against the door . . .

THE DUCK POND

Making our way in stages, we arrived one beautiful evening on the plain. The soft languor of the air, the oblique light of the setting sun, the dust of the road, the tilled fields, everything converged to fill me with an unprecedented rush of enthusiasm.

"Ah, Brindon, why seek solitude when there are human beings who ask for nothing more than our company?"

"No need to elaborate. See those roofs? Let's try to get that far by nightfall."

And Brindon began to whistle. I remarked to myself that nothing fortuitous ever happens to me until nightfall; my worst memories are all linked to the light of day. But I mentioned none of this to the coachman, not wishing to tempt fate.

Those roofs, ah those roofs, how beautiful they were! With their inclines, prolongations, overlaps, shoulders, ruptures, resurgings, they had a human grace and nobility. We were moved at the sight of them, clustered as they were at the mouth of a flowering valley I had overlooked a few weeks earlier. How had these roofs escaped me?

"Did you notice them before, Brindon?"

"Regardless, here we are."

Pigeons were cooing under the eaves, blue smoke was rising from the chimneys, blackbirds were circling as they called out with joy. I couldn't make up my mind to leave my seat, comforted as I was by the tranquility of this rustic scene. The walls took on apricot hues, the little gardens were ablaze with asters and gladiolas. Trees trained themselves good-naturedly against enclosures where sleeping watering cans, their work complete, dreamed of vegetables never before imagined. The doors of the barns and haylofts had been closed, the ploughs had been pushed under their metal sheds; there was straw in front of the stables from the freshly changed litters. Now is the hour of the pumpkins. Look at them gleam and swell in the sun's dying flames; you might call them the stars of the dung heaps. The absence of ducks would have been felt—but they were there, dabbling in the sludge one last time before they went off and made love.

"Because they do make love, don't they?"

"Who?"

"Ducks."

"Let's get serious, shall we? I suggest we go to the village hall and inquire about a good room . . ."

"We could just knock at the first door like we usually do."

As I sat writing this scene, something struck me, which I then remarked to Brindon, namely that I approached each of our adventures the same way: night is falling, we don't know where to sleep, we turn to the first person we come across. "Of course, because it's true," Brindon replied. He didn't understand what I was getting at. It was true, of course, every night we had to sleep, but why this need to say so each time? I concluded that my perceiving every situation in the same way after-the-fact must point to some particular anxiety or obsession. "Probably a remnant of your bourgeois upbringing," said the coachman without malice. I was not convinced.

At any rate, we were just about to knock at a door when a man appeared on the doorstep. Before we could even ask, he offered us accommodation; we had only to make ourselves at home, and his stable boy would take care of the horse and carriage.

"A bourgeois upbringing isn't all bad, you see," I murmured in the coachman's ear.

"Wrong," he retorted. "That wasn't a question of upbringing."

"Excuse me," I replied, "but hospitality is one of the supreme expressions of a nation's good manners."

"Good manners aren't learned," he resumed, "they're given . . ."

"You can't be serious," I interrupted . . .

We let the matter go, out of respect for our host. At the end of a hallway, he opened a door and ushered us into a room that resembled . . .

JASMIN'S VEGETABLE BEDS

"Over there are the peotes. They're not yet ripe. Once the petals fall away, the heart will be twice as large and extremely tender . . ."

"What a beautiful flower! So decorative. I wouldn't have thought it could be edible. And that one?"

"That's a jollz, they blanket the valley. We use them in our armoires for their fragrance."

Brindon and I were in the company of Jasmin, our host from the day before, in his garden of vegetable beds. An adorable little sun dallied among the leaves and it warmed us deliciously.

"Some beautiful lettuce over here," I said.

"That's prapra. It's not edible, but it's necessary for the coulet you see over there. Coulet only thrives next to prapra. We use it as a condiment . . ."

"Charming indeed! So friendship exists between vegetables?"

"Apparently, sir. Curiously enough, if prapra is seasoned with coulet, it's deadly."

"And not otherwise?"

"No. But it has an unpleasant taste, we never eat it."

"How mysterious our vegetable brothers are!"

"This, which resembles your sorrel, is mollon. Poor families use it in place of meat. They chop it up and mix it into wheat flour to make thick crêpes."

"And this, with little currants at the end of each leaf—how strange! Do you eat that too?"

"That's our national chareppy. Have you never tasted chareppy jam? We'll be making a batch presently, the fruit is ripe. Try a little."

"Mmm, delicious. It tastes like rhubarb. And over there, is that a beet?"

"It's a floge. Good for thickening soups. My neighbors dry it for winter but it turns ligneous, and then I don't care for it. When it's fresh, though, floge can stand in for your potato."

"So you've been to our country, Jasmin?"

"I travelled there in my youth. What I remember are those stands, selling those gries . . ."

"Fries, you mean."

"Fries, yes, that's it. I loved them. I tried to introduce the potato here—a lost cause."

"Do you fry the gloge?"

"The floge, you mean. No. What's more, we aren't accustomed to fried foods here."

So went our conversation as we continued to stroll. Brindon yawned outrageously. I dismissed him with an order to prepare our bags.

"Don't tell me you're leaving already," Jasmin said. "Won't you stay for the chareppy jam?"

"It's just that . . ."

"Oh, do stay, sir. I promise you a real regale, and then, picking the fruit is such a pleasant diversion!"

"In that case, my dear man, I accept. I admit your hospitality is exquisite; there is no greater favor you could do my companion and myself than to allow us to spend a few days"—Brindon pinched me—"a few days in your company. Don't you agree, Brindon?"

"Most certainly, sir."

"Be off, then. Report to the mistress of the house and make

every effort to be useful."

I chose to ignore my coachman's disapproval; the chaste and serene air we were breathing would do him much good.

"To tell the truth," Jasmin said once Brindon had left us, "these old servants are irreplaceable, are they not?"

"Indeed."

"Look at this. It's a giant tarrie. From its pulp we make a velouté and from its leaves, a purifying infusion. And this is a mullwine. Notice how tight the bud is. It's delicious in a sweet-and-sour sauce. And this, you'll never guess what this is."

"Err, lettuce perhaps?"

"Nay, sir. It's fly-nabber. We hang it in our kitchens to catch the flies. Touch it. Sticky, isn't it?"

"Verily."

"And that over there is rub-dainty. A powerful aphrodisiac. You can chop it, salt it, mix it into anything. I, for one, make very liberal use of it."

"You do?"

"I do, sir. The orgies I host here night after night exhaust me, literally."

"Your . . . You . . .?"

"You aren't familiar with orgies?"

"Of course I am, my dear man, but I was a thousand leagues from suspecting . . ."

"Suspecting?"

"I . . . No, really this is all so strange!"

"Strange? I'm afaid you've lost me . . ."

"I mean . . . these vegetable beds, this ambience . . . How shall I put it . . ."

"These vegetable beds . . . ?"

I stopped short and, catching sight of a plant, said:

"At long last, a vegetable I know. That's a bean, isn't it?"

"A bean, just as you say. Do you have beans in your land?"

"We have nothing but beans."

By now, we'd walked around the garden and found ourselves where we'd started.

"Please excuse me for abandoning you, my dear man," Jasmin said. "I must attend to the wines for lunch. A few friends

are joining me, and I would be delighted to introduce you. Do
you know the Duchess of Bois-Suspect?"

"The Duchess? ... I seem to recall ..."

"So you do know her. Perfect. You've undoubtedly heard all
the disobliging stories people tell about her; the accusations in
particular are slanderous. I've also invited Princess Hem, who is
no stranger to slander herself. Certain letters have been attributed to her ... But enough of that. Do you count her among
your friends as well?"

"Yes ... err ... that is ..."

"I understand. But let me assure you, she is worth getting to
know ... Our party will include three young men from the village, simple lads but ravishing all the same. No need to dress for
the occasion, of course. It's a family affair."

Jasmin departed and headed for his wine cellar. Dumbstruck
by what he'd said, I had to sit down on the grass. Brindon, who
was probably spying on me, made his way over.

"Well, well," I told him. "I've certainly made a few interesting discoveries."

"What, sir?"

"He's depraved, puts on orgies ..."

"Who, sir?"

"Our host, dear man."

"Impossible."

Should I say that Brindon's eyes flashed with lubricity?

Lunch lasted into the evening, at which point other roister-
ers joined us for the orgy's crowning hour. Our host was so de-
bauched that no form of vice was unknown to him. His guests
moved between the salons according to their respective and
reciprocal tastes, and it was a marvel to see the master of the
house encouraging each attendee with words and gestures. I'd
be overcome with my shame if I were to describe the scenes I
witnessed. Good heavens! From now on let's be wary of those
who cultivate their gardens.

The next day, seeing Brindon, I asked him how his night
ended; needless to say, I'd gone to bed without waiting for him.
On his lips was that smile abhorred by those who can't enjoy
themselves, because it masks both the memory of scandalous

pleasures and the desire to make them seem, to innocents who will never partake of them, even more scandalous.

"I'm glad," I managed. "You enjoyed yourself, I see. Are you thinking of staying on? Far be it from me to drag you away . . ."

"I'll follow my master's lead."

His submissiveness softened my feelings toward him. That's precisely my weakness, I thought; he'd have resisted me had I forced him to clear off at once. I was mortified by what he added:

". . . But I believe my master's presence is an honor for Jasmin who, as he told me, is fully aware that his games are not to everyone's taste. He is going to suggest that my master tend to the garden at his leisure and enjoy the good air in the daytime, then retire in the evening to his room where the library will afford him the pleasure he prefers."

"Fine, that's fine. You may go now."

Jasmin then appeared and bid me good day. He had a juvenescent glow and his eyes were limpid. In his dressing gown with its leafy pattern, his carriage was that of a man whom happiness has made sure of himself. Without intending to, I compared his face with mine in a mirror on the wall: I looked dreadful, utterly gray, my shoulders hunched, my eyes dull. I decided to make light of it and laughed. Seizing my host's arm, I led him to the garden, as if driven by a singular passion and convinced that the passions of others were trivial.

We botanized. As I told Jasmin, I was making a detailed description of his garden for a comparative study. With the tact that characterizes a contented voluptuary, my host made not a single allusion to the previous evening.

THE DUCHESS OF BOIS-SUSPECT

We're weak creatures, weak indeed. What I took for my strength was timidity in disguise. Dear Jasmin, how indebted I am to this man! Three weeks in his company and that of his friends sufficed to make me a sociable being, so I believed at the time. I was completely unrecognizable. Always the first to propose a game, always the last to lose interest. We threw a round of parties here and there and I grew acquainted with this world of wanton living, a world that seems meaningless from the outside but offers an incomparable plenitude to those who come to know it. There is no quality more eminently human, to my mind, than sociability, a sort of genuine curiosity, which, seconded by experience, induces a man to reveal his particular secret; what is commonly referred to as libertine morality is the vital companion of this penchant for others, an affinity that, by the force of things, becomes universal fraternity. What is the secret of each individual? Unformulated, buried under a mass of conventions, mingled with groundless fears, it limits itself to neither the spiritual nor the physical realm but participates in both; how, then, can you deliver your brother from paralyzing doubt if you refuse to offer the assistance of your entire being? "The bed teaches us more about an individual," as Jasmin would say, "than any discourse." This is true.

So it was that these elegant nights deepened my knowledge of others, which would have been restricted to so few individuals had it not been for my host and our providential encounter.

Under such circumstances I met the Duchess of Bois-Suspect, famous for her extravagances and her beauty—a little faded, truth be told, as she was into her fifties, but her charm was singular. What is charm? In her case, it emanated from a state bordering puerility and agony; she seemed always on the verge of drowning in this society whose bounds she refused but for which she would make any concession, being above the socialite's pettiness. This reckless nonchalance enchanted me. She told me her story in a moment of abandon that she very artfully presented as perfectly natural:

"Yes, dear man, I am a foreigner, born along the outer reaches of the Transarcidoine province, in the little town of Nutre, where the customs, as you're not unaware, differ from yours as much or even more than those of the ancient Ya-Ya. It is inexplicable that our two peoples are so dissimilar, given the relatively infinitesimal distance that separates them geographically. To speak only of the family, we know nothing of the basic usages of patriarchy; married women are all-powerful and, in the manner of praying mantises, kill their husbands after the third or fourth child. If a man doesn't give his wife children, she poisons him after two years. The result in married men, who know they are condemned, is an insouciance, a remarkable liberty, the complete absence of a sense of responsibility, and a very broad view of existence. This state of affairs would encourage celibacy and sodomy, were it not for the fact that our men are incapable of living with women other than their wives—undoubtedly due to some psychic defect—and have no taste for sexual eccentricities. These poor boys can do nothing better than to marry and croak. My mother, when we were children, used to tell us bedtime stories of how she'd gone about assassinating our father. No sooner was her last lying-in over than the neighbor women were already harassing her: 'Don't wait for the fourth one, three are plenty given the size of your fortune. Come on, be tough, don't show any pity. Besides, your husband isn't handsome, and for the pleasure he gives you . . .'; alas, they were privy to all her boudoir secrets. Nonetheless our mother hesitated; moreover she could not decide on the means to employ. Her mother had strangled her father, her grandmother had hanged her grandfather, and she was obligated by custom to change the procedure. 'Stabbing, throat slitting, shooting at point-blank,' she would tell us, 'all of that repulsed me.' Vainly seeking an elegant means to conduct her husband to the Stygian shore, she stumbled over an account of tiger hunting in the library; thanks to some presentiment, she opened the book to the page where the natives are preparing a pit with a stake to impale their victim. She was immediately taken with the idea. 'At last,' she would tell us, "I'd found an exit worthy of Rudolph' (that was our father's name). She didn't inform the condemned man of the torture she'd chosen for him, despite his supplications. 'Do I not have the right to know, dear wife, how I will leave your sweet company?' Under the cover of night, she slipped down to the cellar to prepare the trap, taking a church candleholder with a razor-sharp point and placing it in the middle of a hole six feet across, which she then overspread with a mat of reeds. One evening after retiring, she complained of a vague languor and sent our father to the cellar for a bottle of good wine. 'Your reward awaits you, dearheart,' she told him, stretching out in the bed. Our father suspected

nothing of the reward she'd prepared. He went down to the cellar, fell into the trap, and impaled himself, the whole embod-
ied in one fell swoop, from the fundament to the sinuses. 'For
the point of the candleholder was so long,' our mother told us,
'that it must have served for more impalements than candles.'
So it was that our father was found in the morning by the servant (Mother had fallen asleep after her artificious request), and
the young woman rushed upstairs proclaiming deliverance, as
was the custom. 'When I saw Rudolph on his stake,' our mother told us, 'I admired the result of my efforts; he was intact, so
to speak, and might even have still been alive. What could be
uglier than a face disfigured by a violent death?'

"So I grew up," the Duchess went on, "with my brother and
sister in this old house full of memories. We had dogs and cats
that we raised in the courtyard, following the example of our
father, who was a great lover of animals; we applied the methods he'd passed on to the footman in our selection of breeds.
We also enjoyed the company of a few exotic birds kept in a big
aviary; ten years after his master died, the parrot was still saying
'Dad,' as I recall.

"But it was not my fate to settle down in my own country.
At fourteen, I had my first romantic encounter with a foreigner passing through, who removed me from my family's tender
care and brought me to a city I've now forgotten. The treatment
inflicted by my seducer so weakened me that for a long time I
was like an animal, in his snare, without will or memory. I escaped this state of prostration thanks to Loulou, a sailor who
pinched me, as he put it, from Valentin and took me with him
on his amateur voyages; he sailed in the same way others knit,
out of compulsion and idleness. I was so weak that I spent the
first months of our cruise bedridden, seeing nothing, only venturing out of the cabin an hour a day to lie on the bridge in my
blankets. But what a convalescence!

"We found ourselves in the middle of the Chichi Islands.
Have you ever heard of this archipelago? A million islands,
each more lush than the next. We went ashore here and there,
our heads spinning with pleasures, fragrances, and blossoms
as the big tropical trees swayed above us, and in the delicious

shells of warmth formed by the rocky coasts, we spent entire nights in the water. As if we were their lords, the island-dwellers brought us flowers and fruit, venison and honey. How sweet was the wine from their hills, and delectable the water from their springs!

"My best memory is that of Bachenuzzle, the islet of golden flowers. Imagine a minuscule island, at the center of which are three hills and a little volcano; the volcanic eruptions, limited to a benign sputter of warm lava, are so fecund that within hours the hillsides are covered with golden bellflowers. The natives immediately gather the blossoms, their only source of income. Lazy as slugs, they buy all their foodstuffs from their neighbors, and pay for these imports with the little bells. But it wasn't this poetic custom alone that kept me on the island. The Bachenuzzlings, it turns out, are the most artistic beings alive; even the tiniest gesture is an opportunity to revise their aesthetic methods, simply for the glory of accomplishment. I saw peasants dye their oxen to match the weather before heading into the fields: the majestic teams plod to the furrows in amaranth on stormy days, in daffodil or azure on cloudless days, and in puce or crushed fly on rainy days. The women only wash their dishes in rose water, the swaddled babes refuse to relieve themselves in anything but natural silk. And the girls with their diamond-studded breasts! Just as our country folk pierce the ears of their little girls with metal flowers, budding Bachenuzzlings celebrate the first curves of womanhood by having their nipples encrusted with little diamond roses.

"I realized on the Island of Bachenuzzle that I did not love Loulou. What is love? First and foremost, an attraction of the senses. But it's more than that, it's … My sailor had all the physical gifts you could want and I assure you, he knew how to use them, but he lacked a certain spleen, that state of mind through which we come to wish for something other than what we have, or rather, realizing that nothing is preferable to the present, we wish we could prefer something else. Women appreciate these nuances because they spark their desire to please, as well as making them jealous of something they can't even conceive of. A rival is nothing, but an imponderable, what torment!

Loulou was an upstanding man and as straight as his rod; what
I needed, you might say, was a little slackening. This is strange.
One evening I was approached by a young man whose beauty was all the more alluring in the imprecise golds of the setting sun. I was alone; he courted me with an awkward passion aimed not at me, it seemed, but at something invisible. I
don't know how his radiant gaze passed through me to perceive,
just beyond, the fleeting adventuress who bore a resemblance
to me, as I sometimes allowed myself to believe, while at other
times deeming her inimitable. I was absolutely overwhelmed.
And instead of petting and panting, he bought me a soda at the
snack bar. What gallantry! We went over to a table under a tree
and sat down. Night had fallen. A garland of dancehall lights
wound its little reds and blues through the branches. Couples
arrived and ordered lemonades while waiting for the orchestra;
the boys wore white shirts and the girls blue dresses. Their joy
gave to this minute's delay the calm I needed to face the imminent peril that I knew threatened what remained to me . . . or
which, given my lack of confidence . . . or should I say my in-
stinct to . . ."
   "What's she saying?" I asked Brindon in a whisper.
   "Devil if I know, sir . . ."
   "My dear Duchess, it's getting late. My horse must be dying
of cold; I know you'll excuse me if I take my leave now. Please
do come and see me tomorrow at our friend's little dinner party. Your absence would be most intolerable."
   "See you tomorrow, then," said the Duchess.
   The following day, we once again found ourselves in charming company: the Princess, more beautiful than ever, the Duchess, most cheery — she was wearing a ballerina's tutu and slippers that evening — the Duke already drunk, a neighborhood
virgin, the young Armand Touchebarbot as well as his friend
Colin Fripouille, the cook-mistress, Brindon, and myself. We
moved into the salon for coffee. I don't know who made the virgin slip, but there she was on the floor. She was naked under her
dress and before she could hide her thighs, we noticed a master-
ful hickey in the vicinity of her groin. The girl realized this and
reddened. Everyone pretended to go on with their conversations

and the incident was closed. With the cook's help, Jasmin served the coffee. The cook was on fire, the Duke right there. He put his hand under her blouse. She let go of a cup. The Duke got coffee all over his shirtfront. The Duchess admonished him. He cried out. The Princess attacked an American love song on the piano, punctuating it with a sordid chorus of *oh*s and *ah*s.

THE DUCHESS (CONTINUED)

Another day, as we were gathering hollyhocks, the Duchess of Bois-Suspect told me the end of her story:

"Yes, after my island romance, I was disappointed. My native had too much spleen and not enough presence. I gave myself back to Loulou and we set sail again, finally reaching Port-Mouchi, where my man traded in his boat for a honky-tonk frequented by dockers. I worked the cash register all day long while Loulou served the drinks; alas, he ended up his own customer and no longer did a lick of work, leaving it all to me. I managed to sell the business, pay our creditors, and leave Port-Mouchi alone, with no regrets. I landed up in Vadroliapolis after several years on the skids, and in the capital I met the fate of every poor woman who's left with just enough beauty to be desirable. Tedious, my dear, tedious! The street was starting to disgust me when God came to my aid and put a priest on my path who showed me a little kindness; he had a small inheritance he wasted on girls. I had a very good influence on him, for which he was grateful and made me his housekeeper. The sacerdotal life was about to swallow me whole when one morning, after Mass, as I'm scrubbing the cruets in the sacristy, a man arrives and asks to speak to my master. He introduces himself: Duke of Bois-Suspect. The Reverend, not yet changed out of his vestments, excuses himself for a moment. I look the Duke over, he's still a handsome man; I was forty-two at the time. He finds me not without interest and slips me his card. And here I am, a Duchess.

"In gratitude to my holy protector who found himself without a servant, I sent over one of the girls I used to know, and he's told me since that he's satisfied."

"Your story is quite interesting," I said.

"You think so? I myself find it banal, banal . . . I so wish . . ."

"Why, what a ravishing little flower you have there! Is it a sweet nothing?"

"No, an everlasting, my dear man. An everlasting."

THE GREAT STORKS

First they emerge from their lairs in the anfractuosities of the mountain and soar above the glaciers, their plumage dappled with stunning corollas. A flock of winged silhouettes against a sapphire sky, they trail the shadow of their toes—faint, boreal, tapering—across the snow and ice. With saffron beaks and coral legs, with their necks extended toward other suns, the great travelers then leave the summits and descend to the plains where the villagers have decked out the bell towers for their return. The joyful banners reach toward these messengers of the god of heights, spring rushes back like a cataract or whirlwind with its zenith of miraculous flowers on a continent of abandon and love, and all join in welcoming the pontifical bird.

From the forests come the beasts to sign a pact of wild amity with men; bowls of milk for their thirst and meat for their hunger are placed in the courtyards where the children dance, spurred on by their fear of fur and claws, the ferocity of which will inspire legends for centuries. This is the dance of a newly formed understanding. Which ancestor, lost in the mists of time, advocated this barbaric rite? Children were given to beasts, blood drowned the rebirth of the plains and mountains, but the soaring thieves of rainbows set forth one day and inscribed their triangle of peace in the clouds. Tigers and leopards made a pact with men as if they were housecats, for the bird of births had triumphed over death.

ONE FOR THE ROAD

Our stay with Jasmin was nearing its end. Not that our host had tired of our presence or made such a sentiment felt in any way, but the ambience no longer suited us, Brindon no more than myself, and Jasmin must have sensed as much. He insisted nonetheless that we stay to celebrate the birthday of his mistress, for whom his passion was marvelous. The party resembled all the others, finishing as it did in a haze of wine and debauchery. The following day, around noon, as the band was just beginning to stir, Brindon and I prepared to leave. The Princess, seeing us through an open window, cried out in alarm; everyone mobilized and urged us to stay a few days longer until the Duchess celebrated her own birthday . . . This could very well go on forever. So I invented an appointment, to take place a few days hence, with some businessman or other; we were to meet the owner of a manor somewhere to set the conditions of a potential sale.

"You're going to settle down close by?" demanded the Princess. "You might have mentioned it sooner."

Never at a loss for a lie, I pretended I was doing a favor for an invalid friend who wished to take refuge in the country. If he moved to the château, not only would I have the opportunity to visit him, but everyone else as well. Jasmin was enchanted with my promises and offered us champagne, renewing that old custom, one last drink for the road. I remember fondly the little group clustered around the carriage: half-dressed with tousled hair and crusty eyes, they were nonetheless wantonly alive. Brindon and I were anxious to leave, yet touched by their kindness and countless happy memories, with that famous little morning sun I've never seen anywhere else shining down on us. Jasmin had been so considerate as to buy Clotho a new harness and have our carriage, well worn by the vicissitudes of our journey, repainted in mauve. And so we set off amid shouts of *vivat* and a flurry of handkerchiefs.

We continued on until three in the afternoon. Clotho had grown plump and seemed less enamored of the road. "Ah," I said to him, "overindulgence is no good for anyone; this latest departure has left your master and his coachman at a loss, and you yourself are far less jaunty than you once were." In fact, it turned out that a certain mare in Jasmin's stable had only been half-heartedly put upon by our horse.

Brindon was looking dreamy. "Say something," I told him, "anything at all." He hesitated, then:

"I wasn't thinking of Jasmin, I was thinking of you, of us.

Basically, of all of this. Is there any rhyme or reason to it?"

"What do you mean, all of this?"

"Our journey, our teaming up together so to speak, this pleasure you take in writing from one day to the next. I can't understand . . ."

"Understand . . ."

"Understand what interests you. Is it traveling, is it living, is it the life others lead, is it writing? What do you expect from your experiences? And then, are they experiments, or is this behavior natural to you? I've always had the impression . . ."

"The impression . . . ?"

" . . . that you have, how shall I say, some sort of difficulty . . ."

"Difficulty . . . ?"

"As if you were . . . forgive me . . . as if you were always checking . . . to see whether your collar and your cuffs were clean . . . Oh, if only I could express myself."

"You mean to say I lack spontaneity?"

"That's it, yes. But not always. At times you're too spontaneous, I mean compared to your usual attitude, and then you regret it and try to make good for reasons I don't understand, or rather I don't understand your attitude . . . But is it an attitude? It's all so complicated . . ."

"Brindon, always confide what's troubling you; even if I can't provide an answer, it helps me to find myself . . ."

"I knew it! Something doesn't quite square. Finding yourself! Which means . . ."

"Which means . . . ?"

". . . that you're looking for yourself? That you find yourself interesting? I must seem uncivilized, but I can't help but laugh! Oh, forgive me . . ."

"Interesting isn't the word. It's finding who I am . . ."

"But sir, who's going tell you if not me? Or Jasmin? Or anyone else? How do you expect to . . ."

"Brindon, you're a great philosopher."

"Now you're flattering me. I have common sense, that's all. Truth be told, people who sculpt their own statue . . ."

"Their statue . . . ?"

"I mean the one they'd like to have—that makes me laugh. We are what we are, sir. There's no statue. Just a man whose friends say he's likeable or half-mad, or maybe even a poet. But he knows nothing of it. All his efforts to influence the judgment of others defeat him."

"You're being a bit too categorical. But I adore your candor all the same. We shall do great things together, Brindon, you'll see."

THE PROVINCIAL GROCER

So we drive until three o'clock. Then we stop at a greengrocer's on the side of the road. I question the grocer woman: Why is it she set up shop more than ten leagues from any town; does she have customers; is she turning a profit? Her answers are evasive; I infer that her eccentric location was not of her choosing; it must be some sort of quarantine or punishment. What offense did the grocer woman commit? I buy canned goods and shoes from her. "And string," shouts Brindon from the carriage. The grocer woman has a very large stock of tomato sauce, she does everything she can to push the cans on me. I'm wary, the metal is rusted. "I'll take one," I say.

The grocer woman takes a pencil from her chignon and adds up the bill. The total is exorbitant. I protest. The grocer woman calls her dog. A huge mastiff appears between the beaded slats of the sunshade or fly blind or whatever is hanging in the doorway. I pay. Adieu, dear grocer woman.

"Let's move down the road a little before lunch," I tell Brindon. "I didn't like that dog at all."

We stopped near a lilac hedge and I gathered blossoms for a bouquet. Brindon spread a blanket on the grass while I fetched some water at the stream for my flowers; we would put them in a tin can and fasten it to the hood of the carriage.

As we were finishing our meal, a little girl came out of the hedge and approached us. She was wearing a yellow wig with thick braids wrapped in red ribbons. Her eyes were round as marbles and her grin stretched ear to ear. What vile teeth she had! Big yellow horsy teeth, and so many of them!

"Hello, little girl."

"Hello. Do you know who Palimpotas was?"

"Palimpotas . . . ? No, really, I don't recall."

"You can't, he doesn't exist. And Sirrizik?"

"An imaginary philosopher as well, I think."

"No, sir. Sirrizik was one of our greatest mathematicians. He invented the law of backward progressions, the bottomless well, and the cipher's value. Do you know why you're here?"

"Because . . . In order to . . ."

"To be a bore. And do you know . . ."

"Miss," said Brindon, "do you know that you're detestable?"

"And you, that you're a lout?"

"You'd better run along now, or else."

"Come now, children, don't argue. Won't Missy tell us where her house is, and which village . . ."

"My house? Tee, hee, hee."

And the little girl disappeared in a cloud of smoke.

"Strange apparition," I said. "What do you think it means?"

"No idea. But this is one curious country."

We were in the country of the Wind.

THE ANEMONES

In the country of the Wind, the stories are legion; you couldn't tell them all in a lifetime, or even a hundred lifetimes, and the world itself might very well end before they'd all been exhausted. From the very first word, each story gives rise to an infinite number of other stories, as though willfully refusing to be catalogued. How to describe this phenomenon? Neither the storyteller's imaginings nor the play of chance contribute to the endless proliferation.

I'd adapted a few of these tales here and was reading them to Brindon when he interrupted me:

"They strike me as empty. You could carry on this way forever, they offer nothing."

"But this is folklore," I replied, "and as such, highly valuable. Don't you realize some people would sell their souls for folklore?"

"Well, too bad for them. It seems to me you've got better things to do than aid in their damnation."

"Very well, I won't speak of these tales again."

But the temptation was great; ever since we'd been among the Anemones, not a day went by without some knave plucking his fye, a sort of one-string mandolin, recited us the myths that encumber the minds of the locals. They're unhappy if they can't rattle on and on about them, and numerous cases of so-called verbomania have been reported in which the verbomaniac locks himself up alone in his room to pour out all his collective memories; when he finally emerges, it's feet first, as they say, since he's forgotten to eat.

We attended a few of these funerals. Generally, if the madman has no family, it's his neighbors who realize he's approaching death when he's no longer seen outside. Taking care not to disturb him, they wait and say "So-and-so is eating his fye," which means he's at the end of his rope. When they no longer hear him mumbling from the other side of the wall, they break down the door. The poor man is upright, his legs rigid and his mouth open, like a paralyzed orator. This is a Death Standing Up. As they tip him onto the stretcher, the final words that were stuck in his throat come rattling out. If distinct, they'll be inscribed on his tombstone, rather than the default epitaph "Death Standing Up." The cemeteries are full of these. No shroud, no coffin. The family or neighbors who make up the procession recite improvised litanies about the tastes of the deceased. Children are solicited along the way to flesh out the cortege; they'll be flogged afterwards to better etch the ceremony into their minds. Books, newspapers, any manner of printed material to hand is tossed on the dead man as he makes his final journey. Should there be a newsboy in the vicinity, the custom is to buy all his bundles and free him for the day.

At the cemetery, all the printed material is thrown into the grave. Newspaper is stuffed into the dead man's mouth and set on fire; then the cadaver is lowered into the hole. If the paper burns, the epitaph will be preceded by a + sign, otherwise by a – sign; that's for the sake of statistics, which the Anemones relish.

FLED

Charmed as I had been by the country of the Wind, and despite my thoughts of settling there, I had a sudden desire to leave as quickly as possible. Nothing there was true, after all, and so nothing held me, neither the landscapes nor the people; in the morning you didn't know if you were sleeping or had slept, the out-of-the-ordinary was perhaps only imaginary, you were fooled more by yourself than by others, nothing could be counted upon, and these fantasies soon filled me with disgust. Morbid ideas haunted me every night, and the joy I'd hoped for remained a dream; I even reached a point where I spoke of suicide. Human nature is truly disconcerting; we aspire to liberty, yet no sooner is it offered than we feel caught in a vice. One morning Brindon packed our bags without advising me and I awoke en route, so to speak, in our dear old carriage. Oh Brindon, how miserable I am!

"Yes," I told him. "I believed in possibilities. To be at the disposal of the wind, that master of error and disillusion. Fearful of remaining in place—without fervor, without prospects— I made every effort to resemble a wisp of straw swept away by the slightest gust. But what I thought were possibilities were merely impossibilities, and to be a wisp was merely to lisp, with only the solace of a rhyme. Where had this fine burst of chance blown me, and what kind of storm must I confront? None at all, and nowhere but in loops drawing tighter and tighter, labyrinths I first mistook for noble impasses, but which were only culs-de-sac. Ah, Brindon, the sum of our accumulated errors is great and eventually fatal if we don't name it. Failure, it's called failure. A word we should etch into our minds to kill off all those possibilities; what grand master of the shadowy sciences lured us with the sham paradise they offer the weak? Let us have the strength to turn away."

"Sir, what are you saying? Wouldn't turning away be the worst weakness of all?"

"No, Brindon," I responded in a prophetic tone. "And mark my words."

A SPA TOWN

We stopped that evening in the center of a little spa town. The hotel was on a shady square that served as both a park and a concert hall, landscaped to please the eyes and welcome vacationers. As much as I dislike these worldly sorts of places in general, this one agreed with me after the months we'd spent trundling through the near-wilderness of these provinces. Following our arrival, we had neither the time nor the desire to hang around the square, but how delighted we were upon waking to lay out a program for the day, which was to include long siestas and several hours of walking. While Brindon prepared my effects and polished my shoes, I looked out my window at the plane trees where throngs of birds were frolicking; through the greenery, the red roofs of various pavilions were visible along with the colored signs of bars and dance halls. In an open space to the right, players were honing their game on a tennis court. Around it were several benches where older folk were talking, and on a broad sidewalk that surrounded the square, a boisterous crowd was either strolling along or lounging in cafés and sipping aperitifs.

For that day's apparel, I selected a pink and green necktie that was quite ugly, but seemed to match the moment's frivolous, poetic tone; the clothing we choose helps us enter the scene, if you will, that we're likely to find wherever it is we're going. My old red shoes completed my outfit, giving it that elusive touch of ridiculousness that makes it easier for others to approach us; there's nothing appealing in serious attire. As for Brindon, he'd curled the feather in his hat with an iron and had the buttons of his vest shined; his shirt was pressed and his mustache coquettishly turned up at the tips.

We went down to the lobby where the tourists turned to stare in our wake, which I took for a good omen. No sooner had we left the hotel than the people out strolling literally threw themselves at us in a gesture of welcome befitting two messengers from heaven. It is remarkable how often those who appear to be the merriest sort of people are in fact bored and on the lookout for the slightest change; everything around them happens by chance and yet, as if they foresaw that the pleasure they seek will resemble the other easy diversions they have already enjoyed, the slightest variation in their milieu is like a door to salvation. We are clearly the children of our first parents, and the paradise they lost is not about to be forgotten, whatever people may say.

So it was that we were carried on the shoulders of the crowd and set down in the center of the park under the bandstand, where musicians of all stripes instantly took their places and asked us to improvise a song about our travels, offering to accompany us with their instruments. I don't know what rapture came over me at that point; though I can't sing and have no taste for exhibitionism, I belted out the most incredible blues, channeling all the passion of New Orleans. I blended the nostalgic with the barbaric, the puerile with the diabolical, using the highlights of our peregrinations as a framework; now it's all coming back to me, I had it, this framework, before my eyes like a battle plan, and once a given position was captured, I went on to the next amid my audience's wild applause. This enthrallment lasted more than an hour and, at the end of it, my exhaustion was utter. I was laid on the floor of the bandstand where a young English woman mopped my forehead with a kerchief dipped in an ice bucket. Later on, an old lady loosened my belt and fanned me with her reticule.

Brindon was then prevailed upon to perform. Much more modest than I, he simply hummed a few popular tunes from his country which enchanted his avid listeners. We were invited that evening to a dinner at the municipal casino; the mayor showered us with enthusiasm and generosity, the young people implored us for our autographs, and the pretty women rivaled each other with their graces for our benefit. Ah, how sweet it is to be admired!

We spent a charming night strolling through the park illuminated in our honor; sparklers were arranged along the pathways and gave off red or gold light, continually relayed by other flares or interspersed with sprays that rose into the air like sumptuous chrysanthemums. The young people were impatiently awaiting the so-called bouquet, which, if their claims were true, would surpass everything we'd experienced thus far with its splendor. The moment arrived. Pyrotechnicians busily prepared an immense construction extending into the obscurity of the sky. The entire city held its breath for an instant as the masterpiece was set alight. Swirls of stars and flames rose along the axes to the summit, progressively revealing—O surprise— the outline of a gigantic carriage, a horse, and two characters, Brindon and myself. The crowd was delirious. I expressed my amazement to the mayor, telling him how much I admired the skill of his technicians and the rapidity with which they'd accomplished such a beautiful display. He replied that their talents were less prodigious than I thought, since they couldn't do without the assistance of the candle-squirrels, animals specialized in this sort of installation. I wanted to see one of these creatures immediately, but they were sleeping, and waking them at that hour would apparently have put them at risk.

"They're so fragile," the mayor told us, "that disturbing their habits and instincts is potentially disastrous for their health. You'll have ample time to see them tomorrow morning."

We ended the evening conversing agreeably in the gardens and sipping lemonade. I was slightly troubled by the feeling these pleasures provoked in me; I found them strangely bland compared to other indulgences, in drink or in carnal pleasures. My worry gave way to panic at the thought that never again would I partake of the purely spiritual joy of conversation, and that henceforth only excess would find in me the echo that, deep inside each creature, responds to the call of happiness; images of my orgiastic nights filled my mind, obsessing me, and I nearly left my companions for the city's red-light district to raise a bouquet of brute nature that would soar higher than any artificial show.

THE CANDLE-SQUIRRELS

Much like ordinary squirrels, except that their coats employ the full range of whites, grays, beiges, and blacks. Their ears react to the human voice, and it's marvelous to see these intelligent appendages moving every which way to capture our slightest inflections. Their know-how as pyrotechnician-installers is innate, no training is necessary. The so-called master squirrels also understand the laws of ballistics and chemistry. A simple mock-up of the installation is all they need to assess, design, and prepare; and the workers are busy in no time.

The candle-squirrels are fed with hazelnuts and white blackbirds. They are housed not far from the festival square in a little hotel where an English garden provides verdant repose for their weekends as well as the space necessary for their courtship.

We rented a master-squirrel and six journey-squirrels from the mayor to have them mount a display on the roof of our hotel that would be visible throughout the city, as a gesture of our gratitude. Our little workers arrived at precisely nine in the morning and announced themselves to the doorman; we invited them up and they climbed the central staircase with decorum. As they scratched at our door, the master announced, "We are at the service of these gentlemen." Opening the door, we were surprised to see them dressed in spotless overalls, ready to make themselves useful, their faces alert. We had to wait until ten o'clock to speak with the hotel director; he owned another establishment on the outskirts of the city, where he lived, and divided his time between the two sites. We took advantage of the intervening hour to learn more from our friends. They spoke very calmly about their specialty, each one waiting his turn. We were charmed at how articulately they expressed themselves, with the reserve and politeness that characterize people of modest means and afford the listener a lesson in good manners. I offered them a few pralines that I had in my luggage. At this juncture the director arrived and, enchanted by our idea, gave us carte blanche for its realization, whereby we convened to the roof and studied the particulars of our fireworks display. I had thought of some blaze symbolizing love and fraternity; the master-squirrel suggested it might be more accessible to the crowd combined with a heart, for example; a popular and eloquent image, appropriate for all occasions. Brindon and I agreed on this point and left our squirrels to sort out the details. I went down to wash and dress, then spoke with

the director concerning the announcement of our celebration
that evening; he called upon the municipal drummer who was
proclaiming the news on the square within an hour. Returning
to the roof, I found to my utter amazement that the display was
installed and ready, standing a hundred yards high. My squirrels
were chatting and smoking cigarettes.

"In all truth," I said to the master, "this is beyond prodigious. You should set up in our capital or give performances
throughout the world; your profits would be considerable."

He explained that the tranquility of the little town was more
profitable to him and that the bustle of taking up residence
elsewhere or organizing tours would not be to his taste. I then
asked him why the mayor didn't rely solely on the candle-squirrels, rather than on men who needed their assistance. He mod-
estly replied that such exclusivity would go against the respect
due to human beings, in general, and union laws, in particular.

At the stroke of midnight our works were lit. Firecrackers
crackled, flames flared, and little by little they all rose into the
air, growing larger and larger until, from the very center of the
glare, a heart of diamonds was flung into space, palpitating with
sparks and flashing with golden rays; it circled the sky like a furi-
ous star, then exploded into a million smaller hearts that set the
entire firmament ablaze before dying out, exhausted, at a few
thousand leagues in every direction. The impression this spectacle made on me was one of sacred horror; the vision it offered
was more than diversion, it was charged with meaning. Certain
hearts ill-suited to their regulatory function, too big to content themselves with quotidian comforts, too unstable to maintain the passion necessary for an exclusive love, are fated to fit-
fully exhibit all their disordered splendor before falling away as
ashes, worthy of contempt. Each of these hearts seems the only
one of its kind, as though its closest relative were more distant,
more dissimilar, and even more indifferent than the buttercup's
tiny glow is to Apollo, by the very fact of their resemblance.

THE HAIRY HEART

That night, I had a nightmare in which my heart was hairy and viscous, drawing to it all sorts of defenseless animals, who got tangled up in its tousles, suffocated, and died, whereupon they were tossed out by a sort of centrifugal force onto a pile of cadavers in which I recognized everyone I had ever loved, come to life again in this hideous mass grave. Unable to move, they stared at me with loathing. Bound to them by unspeakable pity, I was also unable to move and kept my eyes riveted to the pile. They blamed me for giving them too much hope during my relations with them, and I vainly tried to remember how I had misled them and why my attitude toward them had inspired anything other than confidence. Had I purposefully gotten to know them just so I could forget them—wasn't I just looking for a moment's diversion in their company? Or on the contrary, had the nature of my irrepressible desire to forget my solitude been masked by this desire itself? Had I wanted to love them, had I loved them, was I sincere? Or must I admit I was the lowliest of pleasure-seekers, the most abject of lovers? I watched my hairy heart shudder and continue insatiably to swallow and cast off; animals flowed in as if it were a slaughterhouse. Only when they had been dumped onto the pile of cadavers did I recognize their human traits.

I awoke drenched in sweat. Was it possible that I had been oblivious to so much anguish, that I had so thoroughly disdained others' feelings? I called Brindon and recounted my dream.

"Typical," he said. "You have, and always will have, the soft, fickle heart of an artichoke."

But this preposterous response did nothing to appease me. Was love the greatest defeat of my life? What bitterness I felt as I looked back, what sadness . . .

We did not stay in the little town, because an epidemic broke out shortly after our arrival. People and animals died within a few hours from a cauliflower-shaped phlegmon between the eyes that sucked out the brain and burst on the face like a sewage pipe; the gases that escaped from the abscess infected even the plants, and we later learned that of the town's inhabitants only three old men survived. Today, the place where the town once stood is a desert devoid of all life. So we managed to escape from an unprecedented peril.

The road leading out of the town toward to the sea was beautiful. The poplars along either side danced in the maritime winds, and we breathed deeply.

"Oh, Brindon," I said, "why does fate assail the innocent while sparing the most guilty? Justice is so unfairly distributed in this world that the revolt of good men is justified. These amiable citizens were the victims of a scourge that, in all logic, should only have killed scoundrels and . . ."

"What logic?" asked my coachman.

THE LITTLE SALON

After miles of diligent plodding, we arrived at a village where a certain effervescence was apparent in the streets. We questioned a young woman who told us that the prefect had just had a son after eighteen consecutive daughters. This explained the excitement among the villagers, who'd all been betting on another girl. The prefect had promised a sensational baptism, to take place the following day.

"You should pay him a visit," said the young woman. "The prefect adores foreigners, and I know the occasion to introduce his son will increase his joy tenfold."

With that, we made our way to the prefect's villa, a charming property surrounded by an old-fashioned garden filled with button roses and sweet william. Since the prefect's wife had given birth at home, it was the dry nurse who greeted us at the door. This dry nurse—we'll speak of her again—had a trivial face and a pair of earrings out of proportion with her station in life: two real diamonds as big as eggs, set with rubies and pearls.

She ushered us into a little salon strewn with dirty diapers; a fetid smell filled the air.

"Open the window, " I said to the coachman once we were alone, "I can't bear such effluvia."

I sat near the window and looked out on a courtyard littered with plows and rusty tools. Brindon, having inspected the cases of Meissen porcelains and tripped over the dirty wraps, was growing impatient. The prefect came in just as I was about to impolitely forego the visit—that is, flee.

"I do apologize," he said, "that you had to wait; my wife, still confined to her bed, was holding a tourist bureau meeting in her room and I couldn't get away any sooner. Please, make yourselves at home."

The prefect rummaged through a pile of diapers for a bottle of aperitif, then filled glasses from a cupboard and offered them to us in the most natural of fashions. I'd have liked to make some amiable remark, but the malodorous fumes paralyzed my glottis. Brindon saved face by explaining that we were weary from our travels and merely wished to congratulate our host on the happy event; the innkeeper would be waiting for us with the meal we'd ordered, upon which the prefect thanked us for our courtesy and invited us to attend the baptism the following day. We took our leave.

"You have to admit it's revolting," I told Brindon once we'd reached the street, "to be so utterly devoid of ideas. Why receive guests in this dreadful salon when a garden full of roses . . ."

"The first law of hospitality," interrupted Brindon, "is to open one's door to visitors, but this tradition can be regrettable, I'll grant my master that."

A BAPTISM

The following day, we arrived at the appointed time in front of the church. The entire village was gathered on the square and the family was waiting for the prefect on the porch. No sooner had the priest spied us from his lookout on the steps than he sent an altar boy to lead us onto the porch among the relatives. After welcoming us, the priest explained that I had been chosen as the godfather; our good prefect hadn't dared send word to my hotel and had prevailed upon the priest that morning to persuade me to accept.

"He's a very timid man," added the ecclesiastic. "Your consent would be an honor to him, but you mustn't feel obligated. We'll ask a family member to take on this responsibility if it inconveniences you in any way."

Overwhelmed by so much solicitude, I accepted.

"In that case," the priest said, "I'll ask you to put on this white robe, which symbolizes the innocence of the neophyte you'll be representing."

I was handed a lace garment decorated with ribbons and orange blossoms that I slipped over my clothing. The priest topped this off by placing on my head a little embroidered veil and in my hands a prayer book opened to the baptism page.

"Now I'll ask that you read the responses during the ceremony and make the gestures I indicate to you."

Brindon gave me an amused look.

The prefect arrived, followed by the dry nurse who was holding the child. We made room for them and the prefect shook my hand warmly; his gratitude was such that I wondered whether I'd been foolish to involve myself and what my role as godfather meant to these good people. Was I in for the lion's share of duties? I didn't have time to ponder the matter further, as the ceremony was starting. The package of swaddling clothes and flannels encasing the newborn was unwrapped, and I saw my godson as nature made him. His hairy little head was as wrinkled as a prune, his red hands were too big, his feet were purple, and his entire body was splotched pink and white like a sausage. I asked Brindon in a whisper what caused these dubious spots; he said they were a sign of good circulation. The child was set down on a special table, then the priest put a funnel on his own head that extended down to his chin. Two holes for his eyes and nothing for his mouth, so that his recitations were indistinct; I was very worried about responding since, unable to grasp the liturgical language, I would inevitably miss my cue to speak. But the officiant was not particularly bothered, and when it was my turn to respond, he hit me in the arm and pointed out the line to read in my book; we proceeded this way for two or three pages until, at the end of a phrase I'd reeled off mechanically, I saw my godson turn the color of saffron and take the shape of a crab. I cried out and dropped my book; the congregation was scandalized by my attitude and the priest had to appease his flock and me in particular. He explained that nothing was more natural than this transformation by which the child went from being the devil's son to God's; moreover, it was only the first phase of the final metamorphosis and I should expect many more surprises.

Next he took a candle and rubbed it against the crab, then coated my godson in the holy Vaseline. We recited not a few prayers, and after eight or nine pages, the crab metamorphosed into a fork, then a wriggling lizard; the animal would have escaped us were it not for the nimble deacon who caught it before it could slip between two floor stones. With a precise tap of the aspergillum, the lizard became an over-ripe pear, at which point the dry nurse broke into sobs; I later learned that she had herself lost a child at this point, when the priest had clumsily dropped it. The thurifer poured a drop or two of Armagnac on the pear to symbolize the spirit's triumph over flesh; a few moments of silence were observed during which I sacrilegiously thought how tasty my godson would be in his current state. The inhabitants of this country claim, incidentally, that a heretical sect effectively dealt with over-population by waiting until this phase to cut the baby in half, then into myriad pieces so that each believer got a slice of the pear as well as a taste of hocus pocus, so to speak.

Then the pear was placed on a holy saucer and exposed at the altar of Saint Chu for the time it took to recite five or six pages; I bungled my responses and drew harsh looks from the priest. Brindon was laughing up his sleeve, about to choke on a contrived cough, when I slipped and caught my foot in the lace of my robe; it ripped open all the way up to the top. Once again the congregation expressed its discontent and I was embarrassed to be such a maladroit godfather.

My godson went from pear to fried egg to kale, and finally regained human shape, albeit without a head. At this point, the officiant pronounced a short sermon on the opportunity this deficit offered believers to preserve the holy traditions. "But nature," he went on, "is always one step ahead and soon we will joylessly witness the reforming of the child's sensorium, that eternal source of instability that we all must bear upon our shoulders, despite the grace of baptism." We then recited a few exorcistic formulae to empty the imminent head of its venom. My godson was whole again by the end of the ceremony, as ugly as he had been before it began.

THE DEAD WOMAN

Shortly after giving birth, the prefect's wife contracted blood poisoning and died. Her husband, Victor, was nearly overcome with grief and owed his survival to the dry nurse, who kept him from slipping into the abyss with artful dedication. She good-heartedly met every need of the sick man, whose extreme diminishment necessitated a complete rehabilitation, of body as well as mind. We are too quick to throw stones at certain women and condemn their actions as self-serving, but their motives are often nobler than we suppose, and besides, the result of their work speaks for itself. The prefect came through his predicament nearly safe and sound; the only after-effect was a numbing of his memory that made him speak of his wife as though she were far away but alive, accessible at certain times, in certain mental states, and by certain means, including the telephone. This explains why he would sometimes dial a number—generally at night—and converse with the deceased, asking questions and giving the answers himself. His entourage grew used to these habits until one day, a bizarre turn of events perturbed the household. It was two o'clock in the morning. The dry nurse, who slept in the conjugal bed, awoke the moment the prefect took the telephone from the night stand. Victor asked questions but gave no answers himself. Hearing a voice on the other end, the dry nurse grabbed the second earpiece, despite the prefect's protests, and perceived a distant plaint. Then the voice faded away. The prefect tried to continue his conversation, but to no avail. The dry nurse attempted to reason with her patient, insisting that some devious subscriber was just having her way with him, just play-acting. Then she tried to intimidate Victor and threatened to make his necrophonic conversations public in the village if he didn't reveal his correspondent's number. He became frightened and admitted he'd dialed a number at random, as he usually did. This didn't convince the dry nurse, but over the ensuing months—during which the prefect continued to phone in secret and no longer at night— she tried all sorts of number combinations on her own, getting through to honest subscribers occasionally, and to no one at all most of the time. She finally received an order from the regional exchange to cease her investigations, which were disrupting the network.

About a year after this incident, Victor announced to his mistress that Germaine—his wife—was asking to be exhumed and reburied in the cemetery of her ancestors, several leagues from the village. Sophie—the dry nurse—who had changed her tune and was keeping quiet, raised no objections to this formality, until Victor told her that the remains to be exhumed were not those of Germaine, or rather, that the woman everyone thought was Germaine had never been his wife; the true Germaine, the only Germaine, was one Mademoiselle Amélie de Nontursac, who had died a hundred years ago and was buried in the parish cemetery at such and such a place.

Sophie let Victor drive her to the cemetery, where he led her to a corner long since abandoned and overgrown with weeds. There he pointed out a stone half-sunk into the earth that bore the name in question. Sophie protested, then wheedled, but in vain; she could not persuade Victor that no link had ever existed between the Nontursac family and his own. He refused to let the matter drop, perseverating until the city council granted his request.

The exhumation ceremony took place early one May morning; in attendance were the priest, the beadle, three council members, the prefect, Sophie, and two travelers who were staying at the hotel. After several hours of excavation, the gravediggers uncovered the remains of a few bones along with a little lead box, which they pried open using a crowbar. Inside was a pair of earrings exactly like those of the dry nurse, who paled visibly upon seeing them but would give no explanation. Feigning illness, she was driven home, and Victor was left to his lugubrious activities.

The mortuary convoy took the road for the Nontursac cemetery; the sun had risen and the day promised to be beautiful. In the orchards, the dewy grass was sprinkled with new cherry blossoms; sparrows and titmice chattered in the hedges. In the fields, the narcissus faded, the peonies bloomed, the heads of lettuce grew greener, and above the farmyards and roofs, the big horse chestnuts blushed.

In his haversack the priest was carrying a good bottle of altar wine. He passed it around and everyone took their morning gulp. One of the council members, a jolly and companionable man, told some amusing stories, then asked the gourmands present for lunch ideas; he planned to prepare the meal at the inn during the ceremony. The party had entirely forgotten the object of this event, which was lodged under the truck's seat in a shoebox, the dimensions of the deceased in no way warranting the cost of a new container.

Along the way, they came upon a young demoiselle with a green parasol sitting on the side of the road. She accepted their invitation to climb into the truck, and her presence made the councilman all the merrier and more brazen. Their convoy did not seem funereal in the least, so the party did not reveal the purpose of their voyage to the young woman, who owned a castle in the area and invited her companions to stop in.

The castle appeared after half a league. It was an old manor house arranged like a dessert atop a layer of flowers. An unexpected interlude that proved jovial indeed. The party got out in the cour d'honneur and left the truck in front of the gate. Mademoiselle Dunu—that was the name of the chatelaine, a penniless orphan who modeled for a famous painter—sent her housekeeper behind the woodpile to fetch a certain bottle of absinthe from Grandfather Dunu's time, not intended for altar boys. A table and some glasses, a few wicker chairs, and our friends settled down to drink. One or two brimming rounds brought everyone's spirits to life and Mademoiselle Dunu, acquiescing to her companions' urgings, graciously disrobed; our peasants went into ecstasies over her curves, and may even have lent a hand with her poses. Fortunately the housekeeper was

keeping watch and sent them off without further ado. They
were back in the truck before they realized they'd been stripped
clean; their jackets and billfolds were gone along with all their
provender and, the front seat having been overturned, the shoebox. This detail escaped the notice of the prefect, who was un-
reasonably merry; the priest easily diverted his attention while
the seat was repositioned. All that remained was the matter of
the billfolds. Where and to whom should they turn to find the
thief? The amiability of their hostess made the victims dismiss
any suspicions of the castle's occupants; Mademoiselle Dunu
was very apologetic about the mishap and advised the party to
continue on to Nontursac where they could file a report with
the gendarmes.

They set off. The young woman's liqueur had the benefi-
cial property of preserving all their merriment and they arrived
at their destination with their faces beaming and their clothes
in disarray. They went to the gendarmerie and joyously filed a
report, then to the café where, as civil servants, they ordered
drinks on credit. Meanwhile, one of the councilmen managed
to find a new shoebox at the dime store and fill it with bits of
trash.

Next they went to see the archpriest who'd been waiting
since morning for the convoy and was beginning to think they'd
never arrive. The head of the Nontursac parish was a most con-
ventional man who adhered strictly to form; when he expressed
surprise at the absence of flowers and a coffin, the party scandalized him by presenting the shoebox, and the burial was nearly called off. The old man demanded that the remains of Amé-
lie-Germaine be placed in a casket. The party then turned to
the village carpenter; happily he kept reserves for those passing
through and had the necessary provisions transported to the
rectory. The wake took place in the sacristy and the ceremony
took place in the church, which was draped in black and filled
with the sound of the grand organ. After their eventful journey,
our friends were no longer capable of appreciating the gravi-
ty of the liturgical pomp and fell asleep during the absolution.
At the cemetery, the archpriest subjected them to an oration of

great extravagance, convinced as he was that Amélie de Nontursac was related to the prefect; as for the attendees, they had forgotten the reasons for their presence.

THE DUNU MYSTERY

This adventure completely cured Victor of his madness. The
prefect invited us—I say us because the two hotel guests mixed
up in this funereal farce were none other than Brindon and myself—to spend a week at his home; I was not displeased to stay
in the region a few more days, seizing this chance to elucidate
the mystery of the theft at the castle.

Reaching the prefect's villa, we had the painful surprise of
finding the dry nurse possessed in her turn with necrophonia;
during our absence, she had found the fatal number and was
conversing with an antique dealer she had known, dead now for
two months. In her dialogue with this woman, she made recur-
ring allusions to the earrings, although it was unclear whether
she was referring to her own or those found in the grave; the lat-
ter pair, which had been confiscated by the prefect and hidden
in his secretary, had disappeared.

Victor was devastated to see Sophie in this state; he knew
from experience that nothing would prevent his mistress from
giving herself over to her obsession, and thus decided to wait
for it to pass. But who could say whether the dry nurse, like her
lover, had indeed made contact with a dead woman capable of
helping her? Did this antique dealer love Sophie enough to desire her recovery from beyond the grave? Conjugal love is the
most selfless of feelings; Germaine had loved Victor enough to
effect the Germaine-Amélie transfer in her spouse's mind, and
this was what had saved *him*. Would Sophie be so lucky?

Two days later I informed the prefect of my desire to resolve
the matter of the theft. My intention was to return to the castle,
since I had reason to suspect Mademoiselle Dunu; once there I
would determine what needed to be done, calling in assistance
if necessary. I added that I had very little faith in the gendarmerie of Nontursac.

I left by train. It was a three-hour journey to Bonne-Mesure, which was a mile from the manor house. I took my seat and had started reading the newspaper when I noticed that a woman in the compartment next to mine was making frequent trips into the corridor, apparently for a little fresh air at the window. From time to time, she turned her head toward me with indifference, but her watchful eye did not escape me. What did she want from me? The man on my left noticed the woman's tactic and, amused, made a remark in poor taste; I replied that his observations hardly seemed founded and that I had reason to fear for my safety. At that moment the woman again went out into the corridor; I continued to converse with my neighbor in a very audible voice, explaining that I was carrying jewelry of great value that had belonged to a noble spinster in the region … My stratagem worked; I saw the woman straining to hear and, not realizing she was being watched, jot a few words down in her notebook. I added, still conversing, that while visiting a castle in the area, I had been the victim of a theft that had cost me my billfold. It was then that the woman smiled imperceptibly. A lead, I said to myself. I spent the rest of the journey spying on my victim—or was I hers?—and making plans; I was about to invent some reason to approach her when the train stopped at the station in Bonne-Mesure. As I got off, I glanced at the scheming stranger who was ostensibly watching the sky as she smoked.

I turned onto the little road leading to the castle, which, with my joyous companions, I had taken three days earlier; this time I decided to go by shank's mare to stretch my legs and clear my head.

The air was exquisitely cool and the scent of lilacs mingled with the rich smell of soil, delighting my senses and transporting my imagination to other lands, other evenings I had known. Lilacs never fail to haunt me, recalling a sweetness now lost forever. I had been in love, I was no longer in love, and on this evening I realized that my longing for those distant years would color my moods eternally. However reasonable we may try to be, I said to myself, however boldly we may face the future, as long as lilacs bloom, their scent will bring back those lovely bygone days with all the sharpness of a pinprick.

In spite of the setting sun, the season's light was still admirable when I reached the manor. I had purposely not informed the chatelaine of my arrival. I rang at the gate and waited. The old housekeeper answered without recognizing me; I had to remind her of our visit. She wrinkled her brow and said that Mademoiselle was away at a neighboring castle. Tempting fortune and acting like a perfect lout, I claimed to have seen her at her window. "Ah, she must have returned while I was in the washhouse," said the old woman, and ushered me in.

Apprised of my presence, Mademoiselle Dunu appeared with the most gracious of smiles and invited me to sit before the fireplace in the hall. I told her that professional obligations had brought me back to Nontursac, and between two trains I'd decided to visit her.

"Have you had any news from the gendarmerie?" she asked.

"Yes," I replied, "the thief has been arrested. Dumer, or Dumler—he's already been charged with vagrancy several times; they caught him on his way into the Cherry Tree Auberge in Nontursac, his spoils hidden under the tattered finery he lugs around in his little wagon . . ."

I'd invented this story from start to finish; Mademoiselle Dunu listened dumbstruck for a moment, then interrupted me with a loud burst of laughter.

"It must have been that old loon Amélie," she finally said, "who spurred you on, you or the gendarmes!"

"What do you mean, Amélie? . . . You know Amélie?"

"My dear man, do you take me for a fool? I'm responsible for the shoebox's disappearance the other day, and it was nothing less than justice for the remains of my great-great-aunt to come back into my possession . . ."

"What, you knew? . . ."

"You're asking if I knew? Do you think she's unaware of how to use a telephone? . . ."

"I beg your pardon?"

"You beg my pardon? How can you feign ignorance when your prefect himself was communicating with her and you went along with the reburial charade? You disgust me. Here,

take these, your jackets, your billfolds, your canned food . . .
They might have been useful to me, since I haven't got a dime,
but taking anything from hypocrites is contrary to my temperament."

She took the jackets and everything else from a trunk and
loaded them into my arms, then shoved me toward the door.

"The bones I'm keeping. Farewell, sir."

I returned to the road with my bundle, which I arranged at
the end of my walking stick and slung over my shoulder. By
the time I reached Nontursac, night had fallen and I was beset
with hallucinations, my ears buzzing with phone calls and voices from beyond the grave.

THE GRAVE

It must have been around midnight when I arrived at the Cherry Tree and knocked on the shutters. A second-story light
turned on and the innkeeper leaned out the window. I told him
I was a friend of the prefect's. After he came down to let me in,
I collapsed on a bench in the entryway. He looked at me sus-
piciously. I could say nothing to explain my late arrival, my attire, or that ridiculous bundle. I simply asked him for a bed; he
took me to the second floor and opened one of the three rooms.

"You look tired," he said. "Good night."

I fell asleep immediately. The following morning, a most ap-
petizing breakfast was brought up and as I buttered my piece
of toast, I recalled the previous day's adventure. It was all so incredible! But I had yet to resolve the matter of the earrings and
remembered that Mademoiselle Dunu hadn't said a word about
them. Therein might lie the key to this entire enigma as well as
a means of saving the unfortunate Sophie.

I returned to Amélie's grave at the cemetery. On the freshly overturned soil, I was surprised to find a small bouquet of
wildflowers commonly called knavermines, an unfamiliar variety in those parts but one I'd noticed in the prefect's garden;
Sophie was very fond of this plant, which she grew under her
windows. The bouquet was still relatively fresh and had perhaps
been picked the day before. I bent to examine it more closely

when a sudden noise made me turn around: I barely had time to see a little girl with blonde braids disappear over a wall. I ran after her and pulled myself up, but saw nothing on the other side except a beggar woman who hid her head in her basket as soon as she saw me.

I decided to find the woman I'd seen in the train, whatever the cost. I paid the innkeeper and left him with the jackets, saying someone would come for them in a few days. I went to the train station and bought a ticket for the terminus, which was Chatruse; an omnibus would be passing in three quarters of an hour, leaving time for some refreshment at the station buffet.

THE WOMAN FROM CHATRUSE

I later learned that the woman in the train was named Madame Ferrant. At the terminus, she took her suitcase and a shopping bag from the luggage rack, stepped out of the car, called a porter, and followed him onto the perron. A taxi had been parked in front of the station since that morning; the driver was sleeping. Madame Ferrant tapped his shoulder and he awoke, mumbling an apology. He started the taxi, took the avenue de Lompas, and headed toward the city.

Chatruse is built on the banks of the Flan. This little medieval city is nearly dead, having no industry or commerce. Not so long ago, it was renowned for its excellent pastry and its riverside cafés; its fairs were the country's most exuberant and drew crowds from all of the surrounding villages for two weeks at a time. Nothing or so little remains of this good life that one often says of a hopeless situation: "It's going the way of Chatruse."

The avenue de Lompas ends at the city wall where a portal marks the entrance to Chatruse. The taxi passed through the portal and had to stop some fifty yards on, as traffic was blocked by several handcarts. The driver got out in order to clear the road and reason with the person responsible for the disturbance: a dealer in ladies' wear who was refusing to move her cart until the police came and attested to her right of way. The driver grabbed the woman by the shoulders and pushed her onto the sidewalk while an onlooker moved the cart. Madame

Ferrant, who was watching the scene from her seat, suddenly got out of the taxi and walked over to the onlooker; his expression became worried as she spoke into his ear. He pointed to a man in a fedora standing amid the engrossed spectators, who only had eyes for the confrontation. Madame Ferrant slipped a coin into the onlooker's hand and returned to the taxi unnoticed.

The taxi then crossed the city and, exiting the Portal des Sous, took the road to Verlange. After a mile or so, it stopped in front of a seemingly abandoned house and Madame Ferrant got out; she entered the house through a half-open door and remained inside a quarter of an hour, during which time the driver twice remarked hearing a stifled plaint. Madame Ferrant emerged with a package under her arm. She told the driver to return to Chatruse.

They stopped at number 6 rue Ancienne; Madame Ferrant paid the driver and went inside her house. Night had fallen.

The driver parked his car then walked toward the Three Halbreds Tavern and went inside. The room was full of smoke; a half-dozen drinkers and a table of cardplayers greeted the newcomer. Among them was the man in the fedora, who got up and took the driver aside for a word at the counter.

Meanwhile, Madame Ferrant picked up the telephone and called Mademoiselle Dunu.

"Hello, is that you, Marguerite? It's Germaine."

"So, where do we stand?"

"It's working, my dear. Just a few formalities left . . . Is Pauline there with you?"

"Here she is."

A conversation ensued between Pauline and Germaine about the driver and the man in the fedora; either one or the other would have to be eliminated to avoid any compromises or blackmail.

Pauline, Marguerite Dunu's twin sister, doesn't live at the castle but visits once a week to file away her sister's bills and appease her creditors, who knock at the door with new notices. "Come back on Thursday," says Marguerite, "Pauline will find us a solution." As for the arrangements between creditors and debtors, this isn't the place to discuss them.

I was unaware of Pauline's existence and her collusion with Madame Ferrant. The evening I arrived in Chatruse, unable to find a hotel, I went to the Three Halbreds to make some enquiries; shortly after I ordered a drink at the counter, the driver came in. His discussion with the man in the fedora tipped me off; I approached the two rogues and easily made their acquaintance after buying a few rounds. Once they trusted me, I had no trouble getting them to talk. They knew little about the affair they'd gotten themselves into, but they did mention Madame Ferrant — I felt sure she could be none other than the woman in the train. Then they spoke of her house in Chatruse and her dealings with the "demoiselles," their way of referring to the Dunu sisters.

I did not sleep at all that night. First I wandered through the city turning over endless plans, then I located number 6 rue Ancienne, where I decided to knock at around ten the next morning. In the meantime, I went down to the edge of the river and stretched out on the grass; dawn surprised me as I was about to doze off. I got up with a dull ache in my back. After a few calisthenics on the riverbank, I returned to the Three Halbreds for my morning coffee. When the manager saw me, he looked suspicious and asked if I worked for the police; my pair of drinkers had clearly said too much after I'd left. No, I told him, I had ties to a real estate agency in Verlange looking to invest in neighboring communities. Having learned that Madame Ferrant owned her townhouse, I wished to contact her.

"Well if that's all," said the manager, "I can introduce you. She and I have known each other a long time."

I readily accepted; his recommendation would make the woman more amenable. The manager said he happened to be driving to Verlange for supplies, and that he could take me with him and leave me in Chatruse at Madame Ferrant's; the introductions wouldn't take long.

"But let's wait until nine thirty, ten o'clock," he added. "She's never up any earlier, and I have plenty to do until then."

"I was going to suggest as much," I replied. "My intention was to wait until ten o'clock."

It was only seven thirty. I settled down in a corner of the café and asked Monsieur Legoitre—the manager—to call me when he was about to leave. I instantly fell asleep and was much refreshed when I took my seat in the car two hours later. We reached the rue Ancienne in just a few minutes; I put the time to good use by briefly questioning Legoitre about Madame Ferrant.

"She's all wool and a yard wide," he told me.

THE CASTLE OF BONNE-MESURE

As I was playing policeman in Chatruse, my friend Brindon decided to join me at Bonne-Mesure; knowing I was prone to anxiety and inept at dissimulation—a skill required by my role—he hoped to assist me with his council. He was not unhappy to leave the prefect's villa, as the otherworldly atmosphere of Sophie's company irritated him. So he took the train, as I had, and got off at Bonne-Mesure a few days after I'd left.

He'd already started down the little road to the castle with his suitcase in hand when a peasant passed him and offered to carry his luggage. Brindon accepted and the two men conversed as they walked. Upon learning that Brindon was headed for the manor house, the peasant, whose name was Serinet, took on a wise expression and claimed he knew its story better than anyone. Without further ado, he imparted his singular knowledge:

"The castle of Bonne-Mesure, sir, is what can rightfully be called historic. I never knew the grandfather of the demoiselles Dunu, but my father knew him well and heard him tell scores of anecdotes about the family and their residence. As you will see, the castle retains nothing of the character it once possessed. A fortress it was, sir, and by that I mean a structure built to resist enemy attack. It is said that during the Ya-Ya invasions, Bonne-Mesure, then known as Benemituri, was besieged for six months until the invaders lost interest. Of the three hundred and some besieged, only eighteen remained; they'd devoured each other. To reward such a feat, the king made the castellan—a certain Ménaric in those days—his Grand Huntsman and exonerated him from all royal taxes. The castle then entered into a period of prosperity. Its size was doubled and the surrounding lands were extended beyond Verlange to the west, and as far as Nontursac to the east. Ménaric Dunu divided his time between his employment at court and his labors at Bonne-Mesure. Then one day he froze on his horse during a snowstorm and made the great crossing over, as the expression goes.

"Ménaric's son, Choulas, was not permitted by the king to carry on his father's duties; he drank. Throughout his life he rarely left Bonne-Mesure, and the castle, with the invasions over and the country pacified, became a meeting place for drunkards. The Marquis of Bonne-Mesure, as Choulas dubbed himself (paying his obeisance to the fad of Frenchifying barbarian names), had the good fortune of receiving a far warmer welcome from the king's son, who saw him as the ideal partner in turpitude—he drank as well—and named him, upon acceding to the throne, his Grand Cupbearer. As the Marquis refused to leave his residence, the king joined him there, along with his entourage, and did not budge from Bonne-Mesure unless a letter called him back to his capital for an affair of State. The Queen Mother presided over the regency during her son's spirituous interludes, if you will. As it happened, Queen Alfonsa was one of the sorriest figures of her time; suffering from paranoia and hemophilia, she was manipulated by her physician Truncus and subjected to various experiments, most of which proved disastrous for the kingdom. For example, who hasn't heard of the tax on ears? Any ear that exceeded the format tolerated by the royal edict was taxed in proportion to its measurements, unless the unfortunate possessor donated an ear to the treasury, to be used as fertilizer on red tape plantations; so it was that an increasing number of subjects truncated their ears—*truncated*, from the name Truncus. You've no doubt heard the expression 'to listen with only one ear,' which quickly became popular in these parts.

"The physician was in fact the kingdom's sole ruler for nearly twenty years. This explains the myriad problems that developed, the ramifications of which are still affecting our civil affairs today.

"To return to the castle, in its dungeons are unexplored oubliettes said to hold the mortal remains of certain characters who haunt the minds of our good folk to this day. Take, for instance, Duke Philippe, a lifelong friend of Choulas and collector of his mistresses' pinkies. Whenever a lady would sacrifice her honor to the Duke, he would cut off her little finger and grind the rest of her up into mincemeat. The Marquis had a fatal falling out with the Duke after a massacre of this sort; one of the victims was a distant relative of his closest lady friend. Other enemies of the Dunus included Father Budgebottom, Sir Saillie the Knight, Mademoiselle Hot-Cough, Mother Mastic, and Braille the Lawyer—all of whom were imprisoned for eternity in the Bonne-Mesure dungeons. Incidentally, when I speak of unexplored oubliettes, I merely express the commoner's view. As for myself, I wouldn't be surprised if the Dunu sisters went down into the remotest nooks from time to time and were perfectly familiar with their residuum, which admittedly is no longer incriminating but stands as proof of their ancestors' zeal. For Choulas was far from the only one in his family to engage in disorderly conduct; most of his descendents were involved in scandals, right down to Gaston Dunu, the father of these two demoiselles as well as an inveterate drunk. He set tongues wagging across the land when I was a child and died in a ditch at age thirty-eight on top of a little girl he had strangled.

"But I've gone on and on . . . Might I ask, in fact, what brings you to the castle?"

"I'm to meet my master there, sir, who has business of some sort with these demoiselles, a matter I know nothing about."

"And I suspect you never will, as you seem so discreet . . ."

"I am not of the opinion that a servant may permit himself to breach the rules of propriety with regard to his master," interrupted Brindon who, subtle as ever, wasn't easy to ensnare.

"Very well, sir. Allow me, then, to go on bending your ear, as they say . . . Look, you can see one of the castle's towers from here. It's the Tower of Love, named in memory of Araminte de Folalier, third favorite of Antonin Dunu, Baron of Nontursac and Lord of Verlange, Marquis of Bonne-Mesure. Araminte, widow of the Marshal Duke of Grossou and remarried to the

Count of Folalier, was a beautiful person, one of the most beautiful in the land. The Marquis was presented to her during a ball held by the Dowager of Aircules, and on this very evening their liaison began, a story rich with drama of every sort. Araminte had three children by the Marquis and smothered them in their cribs; they are probably buried in the dungeons. The Countess — in fact separated from her valetudinarian husband, who had suffered a serious wound during battle and never fully recovered — took up residence at Bonne-Mesure where her lovers were so numerous they eventually devised a system of shift rotations. Much to the chagrin of the Marquis, who could do naught but groan when Araminte's lovers would come by turns to her apartment, soon roundly considered the most dizzying of havens. One evening, when Sir Saillie had gone to see his mistress, the Marquis walked in on them, having mixed up his days. A sudden rage made him fly at the young man. Naked as a jaybird, Sir Saillie rushed into the stairwell; only he hadn't figured on the Marquis's faithful valet, who blocked his path and battered him against the steps. From the highest window, Araminte, mad with grief, threw herself into the moat and drowned. That very day, the Marquis locked the fatal tower, eventually having it walled off. He devoted the rest of his life to charitable works and the most ferocious piety, being Spanish by his maternal grandfather.

"The story of Mademoiselle Hot-Cough and Mother Mastic is older, dating from the time of Louis Dunu, advisor to King Guillaumet.

"Theirs were the days of palfreys and ermine-trimmed robes. Babette Hot-Cough, lady-in-waiting to the Marquise, was a young woman of accomplishment in every respect. By upbringing as well as by birth, she was destined to become one of the premier ladies of the kingdom. Moreover, she was still a virgin at eighteen, a condition far from commonplace. The most flattering suitors surrounded her with their assiduities, but to each of her admirers the demoiselle was wont to say: 'I shall not listen to you, handsome sire, until a certain wound from which I suffer has been healed.' The nobility of the day, practiced at solving riddles in the witty ambience of the salons, were

nonetheless perplexed by Babette's enigma, and all the more so
since even the famous apothecaries and physicians sent to treat
her met with the same response. Her condition was beginning
to seem hopeless when, one day, the young and valiant Baron
of Braquard, bound for the Holy Land to do penitence, was
passing through this province and heard talk of the demoiselle.
Craftier than our compatriots, he scented what lay behind the
mystery and resolved to cure the patient. This demanded great
cunning and skill, since for some time the innocent had refused
to let herself be approached by anyone not of her sex. Braquard
thus disguised himself as an old hag, stooping and hobbling,
his limbs quaking like aspen leaves in the wind. He moved into
a hovel near the castle, on the edge of the woods, and to become known for the healing gifts he purported to possess, he
went to the village each day, never failing to fill his basket with
all sorts of plants and ointments made from tother. As chance
would have it, a witch hazel leaf slipped into the composition
of one of these balms and eased the varicose veins of a woman in the village; news quickly spread and Mother Mastic, as
she was called, was soon being sent every case of varicose veins,
pimples, and purulence in the canton. The old hag's reputation
reached the ears of Mademoiselle Hot-Cough who, when the
healer called at the manor house, put up no resistance to being
examined by her.

"You can guess what happened next: innumerable caresses
that the cunning hag insisted were required by the severity of
the wound; and of this wound you can also guess the essence,
as well as the manner in which our knight, tossing off his rags
and brandishing his instrument, cured the patient. She found
herself congruously taken, no time to sigh in relief. Her wound
gaped more than ever, which displeased her not at all, so they
say.

"After this affair, the lady-in-waiting so abandoned herself
to impropriety that there wasn't a stable boy or soldier who
hadn't been her physician, such that the Marquise of Bonne-
Mesure deemed the only cure Babette required was to no longer need one at all; she locked her in the dungeons, along with
Braquard, the cause of so much turmoil, and neither were ever

heard from again."

"The medieval redolence of your story is not lost on me," Brindon said, "and I'm eager to hear about the priest known as Budgebutton."

"It's Budgebottom, sir. I don't honestly know if I can tell that tale, for it's among the most indelicate . . ."

"Go on, sir. You've told a few indelicate tales already."

"Well then, here it is. No sooner had the young Mathurin Ficelle finished his studies at the seminary in Agapa than he was sent by his bishop to the parish of Gea, a village in Parentin. As to when this story takes place, I can't say for certain, though I might situate it alongside mail coaches, foot straps, and crinolines. The adolescent Mathurin was considered—unanimously, in fact—to have the most logical mind and the most unflappable temperament. Of peasant stock, he relied on good sense rather than brilliant intellectual faculties and conducted his work without a hitch, but also without panache. A workhorse, in today's parlance. Never adrift, and totally lacking in whimsy.

"So it was that the Monsignor, impressed by these qualities, had no qualms about assigning him to this vacancy in Gea, as much to test the young man as to obviate his lack of personnel. The death of Gea's aged priest had disconcerted his flock, which during the interim neglected its religious duties and reignited certain neighborhood disputes that the deceased had taken great pains to quell. The parish needed an energetic pastor who wasn't overly meditative and above all, was no stranger to peasant mentalities, by dint of his own upbringing. Mathurin was a good find in every way, even though he had never served as a curate and might well be undermined by his extreme youth. But necessity makes law and Monsignor had made his decision.

"So it was that on a beautiful morning in October, Mathurin arrived in Gea where the atmosphere of the village pleased him at once. He was reminded of scenes from his tender youth and the fresh air he inhaled gave his cheeks a rosy glow. What a charming priest he'll make, thought the girls as he passed, and he greeted them without malice, offering to each and every one his most candid smile. Finding his lodgings was not difficult in the least; straight for the bell tower he flew like a swallow, his

heart rejoicing and his head abuzz with the holy words of the Te
Deum. A short prayer in the church, a loving glance at the Tab-
ernacle, and Mathurin was already ringing at the rectory door,
suitcase in hand. Mademoiselle Bertha ran to let him in, her
eyes round with surprise at the sight of this angelic young man,
whom she kissed on both cheeks like a doting mother. 'At least
you've not lost face to wrinkles and white hair,' she said, em-
ploying a barbarism common in those parts.

"So much purity in that, isn't there, sir? My story begins like
an Easter morning, and it wouldn't take much to leave off there
. . . May God pardon me, but alas the cherry blossoms wither,
simplicity is no more than a brief illusion, and everything that
begins with the blonde tresses of grace ends in the rusty clamp
of sin. Mathurin Ficelle was no exception to this universal law,
and the glory of his ascent was equaled by the monstrosity of
his decline.

"One Sunday evening after Vespers, when the last parishio-
ners had left the church and the priest was out in his garden, he
thought to himself, 'During the six months I've been here, the
good Lord has given me nothing but joy. By His grace, I have
a loving flock that assists me in my duties. No defections from
Sunday Mass, all the newborns baptized, no serious difficulties
with the catechisms, plenty of new recruits for the children's
Marian society, a hard-working choir, sufficient alms, and everyone has confidence in their pastor. Blessed is he who comes
in the name of the Lord, Amen. I pray that Immanuel will continue to look upon me with mercy and make me worthy of the
task He has given me; I owe Him my health and my youth,
may He grant me the perseverance and abnegation that I may
lack, surrounded as I am by such felicity.'

"It was precisely then and there that the Evil One chose to
manifest his presence. Nothing but wickedness in that fallen
mind, nothing but twisted thoughts and perversity! In keeping with the sweetness of the priest's prayer and the purity of
that evening in the village, he took the form of Octavio, better
known as Totoche, the lad from Perrine who was the church's
lead altar boy, handsome as a god, full of gaiety, and quick to
poke fun at the Eternal. Totoche was whistling a little jig when

he passed in front of the fence and stopped to greet Ficelle; he leaned his elbows on the gate, feeling the fatigue of his day in the fields. The priest came over to shake his hand and asked, 'Can you help with Mass tomorrow morning? Fifi is sick and Poulot is at his grams' place, I've got no one else.'

"'Happy to, Father,' replied Totoche, 'but at fifteen, you know, I'm getting old, time to think about replacing me . . .'

"'What are you saying, Totoche? Age is unimportant when it comes to our good Lord, and the longer you serve at the altar, the better son you'll be to your family.'

"'You think?' asked the other, a flash of malice in his eyes.

"'I'm not the one who says so, it's Saint Paul in the epistle to the . . .'

"'Oh, I so like Saint Paul,' Totoche broke in. 'He's got guts, he's . . .'

"'Guts isn't an appropriate term when speaking of a saint, an apostle, or any luminary of the Church. One might say he had spirit, or simply faith, as faith can move mountains. Did you know that, Totoche?'

"'Faith and love, Father.'

"'Of course, Totoche. We must perpetually strive for the love of God; it isn't just given to us. We must work for it, make it stronger, grander. We must understand in order to love, as Saint Eustace said . . .'

"'By the way, Father, have you noticed the big crack to the right of the altar of Saint Chu? You'll have to get that repaired . . .'

"'A crack? I didn't notice . . .'

"'Come on, I'll show you.'

"And Totoche climbed over the little gate and led Ficelle into the church.

"The last lights from the setting sun had just disappeared from the horizon, and the sanctuary was filled with shadow, except for a few candles that pious hands had lit and whose glowing flames rose like prayers in homage to a favorite saint. Novenas of our childhood, who can explain the charm of your accessories and your ritual? Totoche and the priest headed toward the altar of Saint Chu, the boy pulling his pastor along by the sleeve. Under a little flame trembling in its copper sconce, the boy pointed out the crack in the wall, barely visible. But so close was he to the priest, in the dark conspiracy of unformulated prayers and subdued passions, that each recognized himself in the other; a look of distress made the vacillating light of the candelabra sink into Ficelle's eyes, and Totoche placed his lips on the sacerdotal mouth, then with his tongue sought out the tongue ordained by the Holy Spirit. Sacrilegious hands slipped into the slit of the cassock, fully confident of their own efficacy, and under the absent gaze of the saint who reproves carnal lapses, Totoche vanquished Ficelle, who blathered condemnable nothings in profane Latin.

"The priest in Gea thereby became Totoche's plaything, then that of Lubin, then Hippolyte, then Clément, Jacques, Jean, Barthélemy, all rapscallions from the village and its environs, and little by little he took on the appearance of those betrayed by some singularity in their moral tendencies, which led to the nickname of Budgebottom. It is unlikely he incurred the wrath of the Marquis, but rather the curses of Monsignor; nonetheless, popular legend has it that he was thrown into the Bonne-Mesure dungeons where he rots to this day with his brothers in iniquity."

"Well, sir," said Brindon, "now you just have to tell the story of Braille the Lawyer, and we'll have finished with our oubliettes."

"This tale is of a different sort; from one crime to another we come to theft, not the least of the transgressions . . ."

"Go on."

"Braille the Lawyer . . . Let's see, as I recall . . . Yes, Braille the Lawyer was one of those corrupt characters that you encounter in the profession far too often. A vile breed, wouldn't you agree? Since the world began men have complained of these professional crooks, while never excluding them from society for good; I'm speaking of pettifoggers in general, without any distinctions, since to my mind their ilk includes so many fit to be hanged that their entire community ought to be considered as a blight on humanity."

"Indeed, sir. Come to the point."

"Braille the Lawyer, as I was saying, was a despicable fellow. He practiced in Hottencourt, a city with a mediocre population, but one that sufficed for his talents, which he applied to pitting his fellow citizens against each other; there was not one household feud, not one fraudulent bankruptcy, not one crime of passion for which he was not indirectly responsible. Up at sparrowfart, Cyprien Braille paced the streets of the city, on the lookout for the slightest opportunity. If a housewife insulted a shopkeeper, if a delivery boy blocked the road, if a driver molested some peaceful pedestrian strolling by, here was our shark at work, goading the housewife, berating the delivery boy, lecturing the driver, in each case adding fuel to the fire until it was necessary to call in the gendarmes in their subdued, washed-out garb—in Hottencourt, they're barely recognizable as the authorities. Temperatures rise, threats intensify, fists fly, while the police stand around and observe. Monsieur Braille would slip into the cortege and, suddenly honey-tongued, would offer his services to each of the parties, usually settling on the one who seemed most solvent. Admirable work, in truth! The good townfolk were such honest people that they failed to see through the ploys of this clown, who got each fight taken to trial and so bolstered his reputation. At noon, he played the game of nice guy, paying for a drink here, telling a bawdy joke there, and further along pumping a hand from which he'd one day extort silver and gold. At night he could be seen hanging about the bars and clubs, dressed elegantly, spouting society gossip and bland niceties, approaching anyone at all and doing everything he could to extract sympathy and secrets, which he'd then exploit through blackmail or other machinations that one might qualify as . . . chancy, to say the least.

"Now Gaston Dunu, father of those famous demoiselles, and whom I've already mentioned to you, owned in Hottencourt—no more than some ten leagues from Bonne-Mesure—a house he'd mortgaged to the last brick but wanted to keep at all costs in his estate. From time to time, he made an incursion into Hottencourt where he was known as Ginger, as much for the color of his wild hair as for his habit of procuring ginger wine as cheaply as it came; Chapiteau, who owns the bistro on the square, still tells plenty of stories about him. Gaston, relying first on public opinion, then on circumstantiated information about Braille's personality, decided that the surest way out of his dilemma was to turn to our swindler. He made an appointment with his soon-to-be accomplice and presented his case; it was a matter of quickly compensating the mortgage creditors without loosening any of his own purse strings. Of course, Gaston made no attempt to trick Cyprien in laying out the problem, as Cyprien made no attempt to trick him.

"As a retainer, Braille asked for the earrings of the Marquise, which were legendary throughout the land, and he obtained them a few days later to guarantee his remuneration. Then, according to the plan they'd concocted together, Braille was going to mount a proper offensive against certain owners whose properties bordered the Dunu house, inundating them with allegations of neglected easements, unpaid tolls, and other quibbles that, in this neck of the woods, are far from secondary fare for legal men . . ."

"I believe we've arrived," interrupted Brindon, stopping in front of the castle gate. "I regret being unable to hear the end of the story, but I don't wish to inconvenience Mademoiselle Dunu by disturbing her at too late an hour. I'll surely see you again some day, and I thank you for your amiable company."

"No trouble at all," grumbled the chatty peasant who resented this rather abrupt end to their conversation. "My pleasure, sir."

And Serinet continued down the road as Brindon rang at the entrance. Only his exhaustion could excuse the cavalier manner in which he had cut the storyteller short, for the mention of the earrings should have piqued his curiosity.

THE DUNU MYSTERY
(CONTINUED AND CONCLUDED)

Brindon at the castle gate and I myself at Germaine's door, although in different places at different times—two or three days apart—were both in the same situation. The Dunu mystery intrigued each of us, if to varying degrees, since Brindon knew less than his master, but it nonetheless occupied both of us and began to take a more definite shape despite the circumstances, almost in spite of itself. In this way, by the attention of individuals very far apart from one another but united by the same passion, what one might call circumstantial nodes of time and place are created or recreated; these seem to be complexes of a raw mental material that is unexplored, available, full of power, and ready to give rise to some prodigious discovery. But this force is merely a chimera, having every appearance of life, borrowing novelty as needed, making mysterious relationships appear between various possibilities, giving depth to certain imponderables, yet never participating in the only mystery that truly exists: the real. Similarly, we endeavor in our room to build an ideal happiness for the future, convinced that we'll keep hold of it through watchfulness and effort, convinced it can only escape us through inattention, which we avoid from one instant to the next, living on the alert so to speak. And perhaps because several leagues from there some dreamer is taking the same action, the famous circumstantial link is created and persuades us beyond the shadow of a doubt that we are about to achieve our ends. Whereas we'll find ourselves one hundred years later in the same room, empty-handed, having forgotten to open the door and go down into the street where fortune was perhaps waiting for us.

This is why the Dunu mystery does not exist, no more than does any mystery other than that of human grandeur; and as I was setting down our disappointments here—Brindon found nothing at the castle but Marguerite Dunu stirring her soup, and at 6 rue Ancienne I found nothing but Germaine Ferrant taking her bath—I told Brindon that we had been wise not to look beyond these banal scenes for a transcendent reality, and to have simply given up probing with our intelligence what could not be probed, for lack of any depth.

What is most curious in all of this, however, and invalidates what I've just said, is that both of us found each other at the prefect's villa at exactly the same time and exactly the same day, and without having planned this, as if our brief separation had never taken place and both of us—although my pace exceeded his—had only dreamed our deplorable adventure, living through it only in our minds.

THE SPARROWHAWK

The following day we returned to our carriage like slaves to the galley and set off toward the sea.

A sparrowhawk I saw circling above us came down and landed on Clotho's neck. This in no way bothered the horse, who actually seemed to be conversing with the bird. I was curious what might link two animals so unlike each other; how maddening that we cannot immediately grasp certain natural manifestations, since our penchant for mystery makes us think of them as enigmas. Was it enigmatic that a winged creature should enjoy the company of a quadruped? Was it enigmatic that complicity should exist between them? It was not. And yet, my inclination was such that I couldn't help seeing something unusual in their harmony, all the more when Clotho resolutely turned right at a crossroads without any prompting. The bird beat its wings as if in satisfaction and flew over to perch on a kind of menhir a few hundred yards away. At the menhir, Clotho stopped and refused to continue; he turned his head to the sparrowhawk and neighed two or three or four times while pawing the ground with his hoof. I got down from my seat and advanced toward the monument in reconnaissance; when the sparrowhawk saw me approaching, it flew from its perch and disappeared.

Three large stones had been set upright; their bases were some two yards apart and their summits converged to form a rough pyramid in which, not without alarm, I saw something move. I drew closer. A swaddled babe was sitting on a blanket, looking very alert. He babbled when he saw me and smiled with a sweet, toothless grin. What a discovery! I shouted to Brindon that I'd found him a son and, stepping under the pyramid, swooped up the child who continued to delight me in a thousand ways. I took my bundle back to the carriage. At the sight of this unexpected progeniture, the coachman laughed heartily.

"The very thing we needed," he said. "What are we going to

do with this baby?"

"We're going to find him a mother in the next village," I replied. "A motherless child left under a rock is contrary to good hygiene, wouldn't you agree?"

"A timely remark. I was worried your maternal feelings would turn this infant into our traveling companion."

"Come along, let's be off. If memory serves, we should reach Hottencourt in two or three hours."

The baby wore a gold chain around his neck and a medal engraved with the name Gypsophile; on the other side of the medal was a sparrowhawk. Uh-oh, I thought, beware of hasty conclusions. He was quite neatly dressed, as far as I could judge, and seemed to relish my attentions. I have never liked babies, but this one, and not because I'd invented him, was touching in his confidence in me, his dependence on us; were the roles reversed, I'd have been quite content that someone had rescued me from my predicament beneath the menhir, and this idea alone compelled me, as an adult, to do for this unfortunate infant what I would have wanted done for myself. Then I was struck by a sudden anxiety: Would we have to suffer the nauseating chore of changing this child? I put the question to Brindon who erupted with laughter yet again and replied that we'd have plenty of time for that when the circumstances demanded it. I prayed to God that said circumstances would delay their demands until Hottencourt, and settled Gypsophile against the cushions next to me.

"Make sure he doesn't pitch forward headfirst," said the coachman. "A baby is extremely soft and sensitive to the slightest jolt; lean him back a bit."

Which I did. But Gypsophile began to cry like a little devil. So I held him on my knees and bounced him gently. The child was in heaven.

Before long we had to stop, because two bodies lying across the road blocked our way. The faces of the cadavers, a man and a woman, both showed signs of blows and scratches. I looked up and saw the sparrowhawk gliding high in the sky; no connection necessarily existed between the bird's presence and the inert bodies, but for an instant I was tempted to make one. I asked the coachman whether he thought it opportune to take a lock of hair from the cadavers; he saw no reason for this. So we dragged the bodies to the side of the road and were about to climb back into the carriage when it occurred to me to retrieve the man's shirt and shoes; he'd no longer use them and I was in need. As I undressed the corpse, I saw that he wore the same chain around his neck with the same medal as the child. Curious, I looked to see if the woman had one too and saw that she did.

"Without a doubt," I said to Brindon, "these poor people were Gypsophile's parents. I wonder what the sparrowhawk on their amulet means."

"Take the medals," advised the charioteer. "We may have occasion to learn more about these people."

I detached the chains from the necks of the deceased and took my seat next to the orphan. We set off at a trot.

Our progress was once again interrupted by a brownish mass in the middle of the road. This time Brindon stepped from the carriage and cried out in surprise. The obstacle was a pile of dead sparrowhawks, methodically stacked with their heads under their wings so that at first we couldn't identify them.

"These coincidences are a nuisance," I said. "They seem to impel us back to a primitive mentality whereby each event is the manifestation of a supraterrestrial order. I'd made up my mind to . . ."

"Help me throw these feathered bipeds into the ditch."

We arrived in Hottencourt as night was falling; Gypsophile had wailed incessantly for over an hour, despite every ingenuity with which I'd tried to distract him. Who would want the orphan in the village, and how would we explain his presence in our carriage? We'd be taken for kidnappers and complications of all sorts would set in. Fortunately, Brindon hit on the idea of inviting a Gypsy woman to ride in our carriage and pretend to be the child's mother, in return for payment or rather the promise of payment. We could say that we met her en route and offered to convey mother and son, since they had missed the train in Verlange. The woman, unknown in those parts, was happy to play along without further explanation and advised us to take her to a certain inn, which she knew to be frequented by people of her race during their visits to Hottencourt.

"It's managed by a fellow named Chapiteau," she told us.

The name Chapiteau seemed to ring a bell for Brindon. But that didn't matter; the most important thing was to get rid of the baby.

We easily found the inn on the village square. I got out with the Gypsy and went to speak to Chapiteau who was behind his bar in the ground-level café. I paid him the price of a meal and one night's lodgings for the mother and her child, and promised to return the following day; we were expected elsewhere. I got back in the carriage and advised Brindon to take us far from Hottencourt; if we stayed, the Gypsy woman would surely find us the next day and demand the sum we'd promised her, whereas we could barely provide for our own needs and no longer considered ourselves responsible for the child's life. We'd found him a mother far more able than we were to manage the situation, and she was getting free accommodations out of the deal. Brindon acquiesced to my reasoning and we decided to go to the village of Crachon, which was two leagues away.

As we traveled, I considered how nonchalant we'd become, nearly to the point of dishonesty; the same thoughts must have filled Brindon's mind because suddenly:

"No feelings," he said aloud.

And whipped the horse.

CRACHON, OR EXPERIENCE

The town of Crachon is dirty—little maintenance, no garbage collection, and utter complacency with regard to excrement. One doesn't realize the amount of waste and fecal matter a little town can accumulate in the course of, say, a year. In Crachon, these materials are heaped up along the side of the road, not because of any concerns about hygiene, but merely to allow the town's inhabitants to circulate, as in winter when snow is shoveled into banks; one can readily imagine the decorative effect!

We ended up in one of these heaps—Clotho, the carriage,

Brindon, and I—coming upon it in the darkness at a brisk trot; the horse's swerving halt threw us into the mound, and it was with great difficulty that we extracted the carriage, then scraped the mess off our clothes at a fountain. Fortunately the temperature was mild and we took up our quarters for the night in the first shack we found; it would have been awkward to approach anyone at all in our sorry state.

Early the next morning, besmeared as we were, we had no choice but to swallow our pride and ask a farmer for help. Not only did this good man seem unsurprised; he reassured us that accidents like ours happened daily, to tourists but also to locals; he himself was extremely dirty, having slipped the day before into a manure pit . . .

"Really," Brindon said to me when he saw I was setting down our adventure in Crachon, "you choose your episodes poorly. Why speak of this village when so many other memories spring to mind? Incidentally, I miss our philosophical discussions; not so long ago I criticized your penchant for them, but now I wouldn't mind a little divagation."

"Oh, you know," I replied, "Crachon or my philosophy, it's mumbo jumbo either way."

"In any event," he went on gaily, "better words than . . ."

"You may be right. In which case, why don't we talk about experience? What do you think of the experience of others?"

"They say it's useless."

"They speak rashly, my dear man. I'm of the opinion that the experience of others in no way exempts us from having our own, but instead serves to confirm it; I mean that if our investigations bring a certain result to light, we will be assured of its value and follow the course of action it indicates, to the extent we know that others take this course of action as well. We cannot exclude these references a priori from our way of living, however unconscious they may be; which is to say we are sociable animals, no matter how fiercely individualistic we may wish to appear."

"All of that, it seems to me, has already been said . . ."

"And far more elegantly, I admit. But don't forget my weakness for the clichés. Ours is an age, my dear man, where adherence to form is not an overriding concern. Especially to those who pride themselves on innovating . . ."

"Indeed."

We were finally, finally on the road to the sea, the great sea. It was no farther than some fifty miles, and could already be felt in the vegetation around us.

FLORA

Lavender-seagulls. Almost arborescent. Every twelve inches, a pair of little fragrant leaves, pale blue in color, cling to a long stem. At the top of the stem, two living white wings extend or close according to the weather and the hour. Under the high midday sun, the leaves' redolence exacerbated, thousands of outstretched wings beat at various cadences, offering the spectacle of a seagull army held captive by the plant's perfume. Blue and white prefiguration of the fields of the sea.

Morning-joys. These are a sort of pink sun with liquid petals. The sap surges along the circumference of the heart, forming a fountain with twelve or fourteen jets. Pusztas of lavender give way to immense joy fields, which refresh the atmosphere with their humid crops; joys are grown or rather forced by using transplantation and the right fertilizer. In its wild form, the flower is dull in color and its dripping sap forms only embryonic petals.

There is nothing more beautiful than a field of morning-joys in full bloom, and how good it feels to lie nude under these little cascades! The skin grows softer, as suave as a whorl of wild rose, and sadness settles out of the mind; you could spend days under these Showers of Youth.

Barcarolles. Light hulls that remain on land, but once the stem dries and breaks, the flower is free to drift. When the north wind blows, the barcarolles scatter over miles of shrubland, calling to mind a Japanese festival. Mauve and yellow dominate.

Softrods. These are cacti without needles, smooth and very abundant. In the morning, they form shrubs the size of raspberry bushes that by four in the afternoon are as big as cedars. At the first wind from the sea, around seven in the evening, the salt instantly lays siege to the delicate pulp and the trees become nothing but skeletons, then little heaps of fibers.

Dog-poppies. Dangerous, known to attack humans. We saw them from afar, in masses on a hill they'd colored maroon and hyacinth. They bark when fresh meat passes. Starlings that swoop down on the hillsides, lured by a color they take for cherries, are quickly devoured. Each poppy has an extendable stalk; it jumps on its prey and bites it, injecting it with a venom that shortens the fight.

Grudge-softeners. Exquisite flowers, profoundly violet and fragrant, pearled with emerald and shivering with desire. They were transplanted to this maritime region, far too reticent by nature to be its natives. Yet here they are, acclimatized like emigrant populations that, born in the mists of the north, eternally dreaming of snow and fine rain, temper the barbaric fiestas of the southern indigenes. The sight of their mildness makes one think of those boreal American women whose deckchairs, by virtue of being next to a potted palm, seem to tie them to the shores of some tropical gulf. A change of scene, a scene recalled. Their loves, once shot through with gangster drama in the age of pearls and whisky parties, are now lazily curled up between the beach and an innocent orangeade, the fever having long since broken.

So it is with these velvety crucifers.

Veils, chypres, cunnings. Small flowers commonly referred to under the generic name of lassies.

Belt-tossers. This is the name given to the andreosylph pomparous, although the reason escapes me. Oblong and consisting of a single petal, the corolla flares at the top like a collar that, when rubbed with a blade of grass, produces the most melodious sound ever heard. A skillful musician could play the entire scale on a bouquet of belt-tossers.

Something like the resonance of a guitar, only farther away.

Abergies. Pharmaceutical plants that smell of garlic.

Charm-covers. These mosses have a knitted appearance. They cover with their multiple hues the acres of rocks that descend to the sea, and the tourist would be hard-pressed to find a source of greater ecstasy than these natural mosaics. Sheep graze in the charm-covers and take on the shade of their pastures; moving from one to the next, some animals end up mottled like those glass beads known as millefiori. Making love on charm-covers is said to increase your passion tenfold and lovers who have abandoned themselves to their cozy allurement have died of pleasure.

Molodies. Evergreens with hairy needles. Diaphanous like a glass of water, the trunk is both magnifying glass and mirror, such that a man lost in a stand of molodies can never find his way out.

Marjoram, thyme, strawberry trees. Mixed in with the unique flora as if to limit the foreigner's disorientation. Nature and her kindnesses! However wild her flights of fancy she spares a thought for each of us.

Rose-herrings. These derive their name from being packed in herring barrels to produce a gelatin that the fair natives rub into their bottoms and breasts, the proportions of which would be monstrous without this method of hygiene. We came across some country women who followed no regimen and had lost human form, so to speak; working nude in the fields, they resembled gigantic bladders.

Waymissies. We liked this sky-blue blossom, a cousin of the forget-me-not that is unfortunately harmful to the eyes. Staring at a waymissie for too long causes blindness; the flower releases a fluid that attacks the cornea. Brindon nearly lost his sight, but was saved by a little herder who immediately rubbed fresh sheep dung into his eye.

This species was named for the botanist Way. A monument to the memory of this learned man overlooks the sea.

Sel-selphs. Tuberoses with human voices. They call out and respond to each other from hill to hill; in the excessive heat of the afternoon, the slow rhythm of their exchange pervades the mind like an obsession. Amplified by the immense corolla, their voices carry over miles and miles; the timbre is muted and mysterious.

Vertigo-missoines. Bouquet-type flowers.

THE GREAT PORTAL

We passed through these regions quickly, impatient to reach the sea. But some kind of fear oppressed me. I was both eager and anxious, as if an event was approaching that would revolutionize my existence, however unready I felt. What was it in me that secretly tried to ward off this surprise? And why expect from my encounter with the sea anything other than what chance had hitherto given me for guidance? It can happen, I think, that a man long influenced by unspoken conventions has yet to begin his life, or rather, having taken up a certain path like those around him, he exists as someone other than himself, unwillingly becoming what might be called the atavistic double; through our ancestors, each of us becomes this character independent of ourselves, an enemy most of the time, who by force of habit prevails over our unique person and may lead us all the way to the grave. Behind its mask we are hidden from all mirrors, and our true face dies without ever seeing the light of day. Since there are several atavistic characters, these interlopers could theoretically supplant our idiosyncrasy and make us pass through all the points along their path, which, like the highways on a geographical map that converge on a given location, purport to be the waypoints of our souls. They sometimes reveal themselves in reactions that surprise us, creating those empty spaces where we seem absent from ourselves; this might explain the belief in metempsychosis: the transposition in space and time of an essentially delimited phenomenon. But all of that is pure illusion; our atavisms in no way hold the key to ourselves. They merely encourage us in our laziness to conform to the habits of our fathers, who may never have in fact existed if they, too, blindly accepted the habits passed down to them. That alone could prompt us to renounce every filiation . . . But I've strayed into the meanders of a logic that is clearly not my own.

Brindon hadn't said anything for some time and I asked

him what he was pondering. He replied that it wouldn't be far-fetched to believe the sea was moving away from us as we approached, since all his calculations indicated we should have arrived already. I said his atavistic double was probably playing a trick on him, and he called me an imbecile for the first time on our journey. I concluded that he was exhausted; his equanimity had not accustomed me to such unseemliness. He did, in fact, excuse himself immediately.

"All is forgiven," I told him. "There's something strangely oppressive in the air; I feel it, too. Maybe we should slow down a bit because, at any rate . . ."

"Look! What did I tell you?"

We'd arrived at the edge of a cliff that had been masking the immense plain it overlooked. The sea, as a result, seemed farther away. But the beauty of this plain enchanted me; almost desert-like and tawny as a wildcat's pelt, it was dotted with bouquets of gray vegetation between large paludal stretches whose colors, at this advancing hour, took on a surreal cast. The twilit sky was reflected in the marshes and, clarified by the waters, seemed to bore through the plain and meet itself on the other side.

Sitting on the edge of the cliff, we smoked our best cigarette of the day.

"You see," I said to my coachman, "what you took to be an ordeal is really nothing of the sort."

"What?"

"You hoped to reach the sea this evening and we're still dozens of leagues from it."

"Wasn't that your desire as well?"

"Yes, of course, but I'm feeling so good now, I've forgotten everything else and my desires are starting to seem worthless."

"What do you mean?"

"That my desires — in this case, my desire for the sea — may not correspond to my temperament. It's once again this problem of possibilities, so disconcerting to me that I can't tell what truly suits my tastes."

"You're making an awful lot of this contretemps."

"Wrong, my dear man, wrong. You have no idea how I suffer from my idleness, it's becoming a most tiresome source of tension. Why the sea, when this plain is everything I could ever want?"

"Because you wouldn't have liked this plain if it hadn't thwarted your desire for the sea."

"Do go on . . ."

"There's nothing to add. You fear your desires, and what delays gratification is a comfort to you."

"So, in other words, I'm a coward?"

"Precisely."

I so enjoyed my coachman's observations. They came to him impromptu, as if from outside himself.

"Now then, explain to me why I'm afraid of reaching the sea."

"Because you won't know how to describe it."

". . . Brindon, you're a genius."

We went on speaking of this and that. The plain turned pale pink, then fuchsia, then periwinkle blue. Like holes in a giant sieve through which the firmament was flowing, the marshes retained the sky's liquid tones. For an instant, I had the revelation of cosmic capillarities and intersidereal currents. Such reveries, however vain, exalt the imagination.

Then we got back in the carriage. The road did not lead directly to the plain, first following the cliff edge, then entering a narrow gorge formed by low hills that I hadn't noticed on our left, where the vegetation was quite different: pointed fronds of stunted palm trees rose up about a yard from the ground to form beige tufts. Wildcats nesting there leapt up as if on springs when we called to them; their pantomime was amusing and brought back memories of the flea circus.

One of these animals lay motionless in the road with an injured paw; we stopped and I tried to treat his injuries, but to my surprise his fur pulled away in strips and lay in my hands like a decaying pelisse. I didn't know if it was better to abandon the animal to his injury or risk seeing him bereft of his skin; the slightest touch exfoliated him further. That's when he signaled with his head several times toward the same area, and I understood there might be a remedy in that direction. I walked about

fifty yards to a shrub higher than the others with orange berries
between its leaves. After picking a few, I returned to the panting
cat. He threw himself on the berries and devoured them them;
then his limbs became still and he lay down on his side. As I
watched, not knowing what to do, his belly swelled, his paws
shriveled, his fur slid off like an unbuttoned shirt, and big blue
feathers sprouted from his skin. His head became that of a cormorant, he was reduced to two legs with webbed feet, and his
body turned into a large bird's. He stood up and began smooth-
ing his new feathers with his beak. Fifteen cats or so gathered in
a circle around him. The cormorant gave a little speech in animal language and all the cats wiggled their whiskers; then he
flew off toward the sea.

I went back to the shrub and picked what remained of the
fruit, which I put in my pocket before returning to the carriage.
Brindon was sleeping. I was almost tempted to offer him the
berries, but what would become of our fond friendship if my
coachman flew out of his seat? Keep those magical kkernels, I
said to myself, so we can put them to better use. Brindon asked
me what I'd done with the injured cat and I told him I'd simply
changed it into a bird.

"Well, you're certainly getting my goat," he quipped.

We were still crossing the valley when the road suddenly curved and opened out onto the plain. Gone were the vast
marshes we'd just been admiring. Fields of mature wheat spread
before us, in the middle of which a sumptuous portal rose
shockingly into the sky. We gazed at the spectacle with our
mouths agape. Clotho stopped abruptly and whinnied in terror. Before us stood a portal in the form of a triumphal arch, so
enormous that the surrounding countryside seemed flattened
by it.

"What's the meaning of this?" I asked Brindon. "Were you
ever told anything about it?"

"Nothing at all. But could it be an illusion we're seeing? A
mirage?"

"Let's have a closer look."

We moved forward about one league into the fields of wheat
and oats. The portal rose over us like the Himalayas. It had been

built in the middle of a clearing, devoid of crops, and we could see that it marked the entrance to a city whose outer districts, Lilliputian at this distance, ended at the base of its pilasters. About fifteen leagues separated us from this structure, which not a soul had ever mentioned. We were also bewildered by its orientation; when we'd looked out over the sea and the colored checkerboard of rocks, we'd seen no trace of it. Our itinerary had then branched off to the left, but how was such a change in the landscape possible? We were surrounded by grain crops under a clear sky that had nothing to do with the maritime horizon we'd seen only a short while ago; even the salty wind we'd felt against our lips had disappeared. Surely this provocatively huge portal was guarding more than the entrance to a city. We continued moving forward. The colossal architecture seemed to brush up against our eyelids as if we were hallucinating. We gazed at the details of its frescos and enameling, its bas-reliefs and freestanding sculptures as if discovering an art we'd never imagined to exist. Three cornices more brilliant than gold crowned this chef d'œuvre.

During the two hours of our approach, we only had eyes for these marvels.

DETAILED DESCRIPTION OF THE PORTAL

Starting from the top, black salamanders are deeply engraved in the marble under the sparkling cornices; rising ten meters high, they seem crucified on the frieze. Alternating with the salamanders are newts painted yellow and red, like fiery dragons, which enlace in their supple limbs the lilac discs strewn along the intervals. Each of these discs encloses a gentle countryside or a melancholy face, whereas inside the newts and salamanders, thousands of strange animals are painted or engraved, hemming in the mauve islands like a menacing throng. The large figures follow on from each other with such regularity that one can almost hear the whoosh of waves three thousand feet above the plain.

Under the salamanders, and separated from them by a double thread of topaz, large daisies stretch their petals against a

rosewood background. Their centers, twenty-four feet high,
consist of brick tiles that bear the names of bygone heroes and
battles, now illegible. Each flower is isolated from the next by a
ring of mosaic whose contour, studded with triangular mirrors,
reflects the milky tones of the petals and elongates them, giving the flower an incurved appearance. Smaller asters shine in
the interstices and embroider the lower part of the band. Sup-
porting it are big diagonal blocks that give the illusion of a tri-
ple-stranded cable; lapis lazuli and rock crystal are thus wedded
over a surface of some forty-five hundred square feet. The layer
below consists of glass balls, set in the granite and forming three
rows of pearls fifteen feet in diameter; inside the balls, caught in·
the glass, corpuscles of bronze and silver form a most sophisticated image of the universe's disorder, an image repeated twenty
times on each pillar. We learned from a beggar that these forty
universes are the steps by which the wise man attains supreme
indifference.

Under the pearls, seven plinths lacking ornamentation represent the seven letters of silence; they are the starting point for
the large banners that unfurl like cascades, streaked with azure
and emerald. These rare marbles are incrusted with mica and
schist; into the solid gold they plunge pudding stones consisting of sand conglomerated around pebbles and representing the
masses indoctrinated by religious zealots. These stones peak in
the middle of the banners, rippling through the marble over a
height of four hundred and fifty feet. Between the banners and
the band of cobalt around them, entangled bodies writhe like
serpents. These are the bodies of the lovers of every past era, im-
bricated to fit their vast numbers into a relatively limited space;
soon they will encroach even upon the plinths of silence, as
love will continue to bring bodies together in the coming centuries and not a one of them will escape the chisels of the portal's sculptors.

Geometrical patterns serve as a base for the sand conglomer-
ates; they are in high relief with an orderliness that calls to mind
the map of an ideal city. Cubes embedded in cones represent
houses on hillsides; hexagons, circles, and trapezoids are pla-
zas between the tangle of parallel curves, broken lines, and an-

gles of all sorts — avenues, squares, streets, and quays following a clear ribbon thirty feet in width that zigzags along a meander doubled back on itself four times.

Below that, a band of fine openwork symbolizes the fabric of days; the studied line of arabesques disperses one's gaze so that it comes to rest here and there on colored points, relays in each millennium until the present day; the points, around one hundred thousand in number, give an indication of the portal's age.

Two white bands cross under the arabesques, consisting of folds sculpted in the limestone and resembling a gigantic turban; they widen at the edges of the pillar then narrow at its center, overlapping like two opposing triangles. The diamond resulting from their conjuncture is the eye of Graal Flibuste, god of imaginary fervors and master of the world; the unbearable whiteness of the stone shatters the dimensions of the eye, which like the sun shines over the entire pillar as the centerpiece of its decor.

Clover mingled with tulips covers three hundred feet in the space between the lower point of the eye and a mahogany molding just inside the framework of the whole. The colors of the flowers, the swirls of the stems, and the elegant branching of the leaves are as graceful as Levantine festivities, where artifice replaces all the seductions of the real world. The result might be compared to dancers who die in the impossible attitude granted to them by a second of ecstasy, who in their effort to escape the fundamental laws of movement are sacrificed, martyred, and finally fulfilled in their delirious wish to invent for no one's glory a new way in which to serve beauty.

Next is a series of *Ss* or joined crescents, a stylized representation of parallel swimmers on an azurite background that is supported by a frieze of carbuncles and mother-of-pearl. They precede the immense octopus-anemone that spans six hundred feet. The full range of golds is blended into the mane of the Oceanic goddess who swims in the lavender waters; with refined brush strokes, they have been streaked with pink and violet gray, giving their surface an iridescent glaze of pastel. The octopus-anemone imprisoned in its rectangle is the emblem of the soul's revolutions stifled by social obligations; this problem is of great interest to the moralists of this land, which explains the casual acceptance with which indigenous artists approach the subject.

Once again the seven plinths, but narrower this time, and in trompe-l'oeil style; below, the last fragment covered with medallions and broken lines which simulate the scallops of a diadem. This part of each pillar rises six hundred feet from the ground and forms the base. It is not as beautiful as the rest of the portal; a theatrical vision governed its decoration, if only in the avoidance of rare materials and the use of false perspectives. A flight of swallows on a clear background invades every other medallion, while the middle ground is occupied by different species of trees, laden with flowers and fruit. Overall, one may have the illusion of a countryside seen from some height that appears to reflect itself, repeated by the mirror image below, in the waters of a river snaking thirty feet from the ground, lined with lotus and black peonies.

ROBERT PINGET was born in 1920 in Geneva. His first collection of stories was pubished in 1951. Pinget has written more than 30 books: novels, plays, and "notebooks," of which *Trio*, *Mahu or the Material*, and *The Inquisitory* were published in translation by Dalkey Archive Press. Pinget's last book, *Taches d'Encre*, came out in 1997, the year he died.

ANNA FITZGERALD is an American translator born in 1976 who lives and works in southern France.

FRENCH LITERATURE SERIES

ROBERT PINGET
TRIO
Preface by John Updike
Translated by Barbara Wright

Trio marks the first time these three shorter Pinget works are collected in a single volume. From the sublime surrealism of *Between Fantoine and Agapa*, through the Faulknerian take on rural life in *That Voice*, to the musical rhythm and flow of *Passacaglia*, this collection charts the varied career of one of the French New Novel's true luminaries.

The space between the fictional towns of *Fantoine and Agapa* is akin to Faulkner's Yoknapatawpha County: an area where provincialism is neither romanticized nor parodied; where intrigue—often violent intrigue—confronts the bucolic ideal held both by insiders and outsiders; and where reality is shaped not by events, but by talk and gossip, by insinuation and conjecture.

Written over the course of his career, these three novels are by turns hilarious and dark, surreal and painstakingly accurate; together they demonstrate the consistent quality of Pinget's versatility.

Available at **www.dalkeyarchive.com**

SCHOLARLY SERIES

BARBARA WRIGHT: TRANSLATION AS ART
Edited by Madeleine Renouard and Debra Kelly

Legendary publisher and writer John Calder said of Barbara Wright that she was "the most brilliant, conscientious and original translator of 20th century French literature." Wright introduced to an English-speaking readership and audience some of the most innovative French literature of the last hundred years: a world without Alfred Jarry's *Ubu*, Raymond Queneau's *Zazie*, and Robert Pinget's *Monsieur Songe* scarcely bears thinking about. This wonderful collection of texts about and by Barbara Wright—including work by David Bellos, Breon Mitchell, and Nick Wadley, as well as a previously unpublished screenplay written and translated by Wright in collaboration with Robert Pinget—begins the work of properly commemorating a figure toward whom all of English letters owes an unpayable debt.

Available at **www.dalkeyarchive.com**

MICHAL AJVAZ, *The Golden Age.*
The Other City.

PIERRE ALBERT-BIROT, *Grabinoulor.*

YUZ ALESHKOVSKY, *Kangaroo.*

FELIPE ALFAU, *Chromos.*
Locos.

JOE AMATO, *Samuel Taylor's Last Night.*

IVAN ÂNGELO, *The Celebration.*
The Tower of Glass.

ANTÓNIO LOBO ANTUNES, *Knowledge of Hell.*
The Splendor of Portugal.

ALAIN ARIAS-MISSON, *Theatre of Incest.*

JOHN ASHBERY & JAMES SCHUYLER,
A Nest of Ninnies.

ROBERT ASHLEY, *Perfect Lives.*

GABRIELA AVIGUR-ROTEM, *Heatwave and Crazy Birds.*

DJUNA BARNES, *Ladies Almanack.*
Ryder.

JOHN BARTH, *Letters.*
Sabbatical.

DONALD BARTHELME, *The King.*
Paradise.

SVETISLAV BASARA, *Chinese Letter.*

MIQUEL BAUÇÀ, *The Siege in the Room.*

RENÉ BELLETTO, *Dying.*

MAREK BIENCZYK, *Transparency.*

ANDREI BITOV, *Pushkin House.*

ANDREJ BLATNIK, *You Do Understand.*
Law of Desire.

LOUIS PAUL BOON, *Chapel Road.*
My Little War.
Summer in Termuren.

ROGER BOYLAN, *Killoyle.*

IGNÁCIO DE LOYOLA BRANDÃO,
Anonymous Celebrity.
Zero.

BONNIE BREMSER, *Troia: Mexican Memoirs.*

CHRISTINE BROOKE-ROSE,
Amalgamemnon.

BRIGID BROPHY, *In Transit.*
The Prancing Novelist.

GERALD L. BRUNS,
Modern Poetry and the Idea of Language.

GABRIELLE BURTON, *Heartbreak Hotel.*

MICHEL BUTOR, *Degrees.*
Mobile.

G. CABRERA INFANTE, *Infante's Inferno.*
Three Trapped Tigers.

JULIETA CAMPOS, *The Fear of Losing Eurydice.*

ANNE CARSON, *Eros the Bittersweet.*

ORLY CASTEL-BLOOM, *Dolly City.*

LOUIS-FERDINAND CÉLINE, *North.*
Conversations with Professor Y.
London Bridge.

MARIE CHAIX, *The Laurels of Lake Constance.*

HUGO CHARTERIS, *The Tide Is Right.*

ERIC CHEVILLARD, *Demolishing Nisard.*
The Author and Me.

MARC CHOLODENKO, *Mordechai Schamz.*

JOSHUA COHEN, *Witz.*

EMILY HOLMES COLEMAN, *The Shutter of Snow.*

ERIC CHEVILLARD, *The Author and Me.*

ROBERT COOVER, *A Night at the Movies.*

STANLEY CRAWFORD, *Log of the S.S. The Mrs Unguentine.*
Some Instructions to My Wife.

RENÉ CREVEL, *Putting My Foot in It.*

RALPH CUSACK, *Cadenza.*

NICHOLAS DELBANCO, *Sherbrookes.*
The Count of Concord.

NIGEL DENNIS, *Cards of Identity.*

PETER DIMOCK, *A Short Rhetoric for Leaving the Family.*

ARIEL DORFMAN, *Konfidenz.*

COLEMAN DOWELL, *Island People.*
Too Much Flesh and Jabez.

ARKADII DRAGOMOSHCHENKO,
Dust.

RIKKI DUCORNET, *Phosphor in Dreamland.*
The Complete Butcher's Tales.

RIKKI DUCORNET (cont.), *The Jade Cabinet.*
The Fountains of Neptune.

WILLIAM EASTLAKE, *The Bamboo Bed.*
Castle Keep.
Lyric of the Circle Heart.

JEAN ECHENOZ, *Chopin's Move.*

STANLEY ELKIN, *A Bad Man.*
Criers and Kibitzers, Kibitzers and Criers.
The Dick Gibson Show.
The Franchiser.
The Living End.
Mrs. Ted Bliss.

FRANÇOIS EMMANUEL, *Invitation to a Voyage.*

PAUL EMOND, *The Dance of a Sham.*

SALVADOR ESPRIU, *Ariadne in the Grotesque Labyrinth.*

LESLIE A. FIEDLER, *Love and Death in the American Novel.*

JUAN FILLOY, *Op Oloop.*

ANDY FITCH, *Pop Poetics.*

GUSTAVE FLAUBERT, *Bouvard and Pécuchet.*

KASS FLEISHER, *Talking out of School.*

JON FOSSE, *Aliss at the Fire.*
Melancholy.

FORD MADOX FORD, *The March of Literature.*

MAX FRISCH, *I'm Not Stiller.*
Man in the Holocene.

CARLOS FUENTES, *Christopher Unborn.*
Distant Relations.
Terra Nostra.
Where the Air Is Clear.

TAKEHIKO FUKUNAGA, *Flowers of Grass.*

WILLIAM GADDIS, JR., *The Recognitions.*

JANICE GALLOWAY, *Foreign Parts.*
The Trick Is to Keep Breathing.

WILLIAM H. GASS, *Life Sentences.*
The Tunnel.
The World Within the Word.
Willie Masters' Lonesome Wife.

GÉRARD GAVARRY, *Hoppla! 1 2 3.*

ETIENNE GILSON, *The Arts of the Beautiful.*
Forms and Substances in the Arts.

C. S. GISCOMBE, *Giscome Road.*
Here.

DOUGLAS GLOVER, *Bad News of the Heart.*

WITOLD GOMBROWICZ, *A Kind of Testament.*

PAULO EMÍLIO SALES GOMES, *P's Three Women.*

GEORGI GOSPODINOV, *Natural Novel.*

JUAN GOYTISOLO, *Count Julian.*
Juan the Landless.
Makbara.
Marks of Identity.

HENRY GREEN, *Blindness.*
Concluding.
Doting.
Nothing.

JACK GREEN, *Fire the Bastards!*

JIŘÍ GRUŠA, *The Questionnaire.*

MELA HARTWIG, *Am I a Redundant Human Being?*

JOHN HAWKES, *The Passion Artist.*
Whistlejacket.

ELIZABETH HEIGHWAY, ED., *Contemporary Georgian Fiction.*

AIDAN HIGGINS, *Balcony of Europe.*
Blind Man's Bluff.
Bornholm Night-Ferry.
Langrishe, Go Down.
Scenes from a Receding Past.

KEIZO HINO, *Isle of Dreams.*

KAZUSHI HOSAKA, *Plainsong.*

ALDOUS HUXLEY, *Antic Hay.*
Point Counter Point.
Those Barren Leaves.
Time Must Have a Stop.

NAOYUKI II, *The Shadow of a Blue Cat.*

DRAGO JANČAR, *The Tree with No Name.*

MIKHEIL JAVAKHISHVILI, *Kvachi.*

GERT JONKE, *The Distant Sound.*
Homage to Czerny.
The System of Vienna.

JACQUES JOUET, *Mountain R.*
Savage.
Upstaged.

MIEKO KANAI, *The Word Book.*

YORAM KANIUK, *Life on Sandpaper.*

ZURAB KARUMIDZE, *Dagny.*

JOHN KELLY, *From Out of the City.*

HUGH KENNER, *Flaubert, Joyce and Beckett: The Stoic Comedians.*
Joyce's Voices.

DANILO KIŠ, *The Attic.*
The Lute and the Scars.
Psalm 44.
A Tomb for Boris Davidovich.

ANITA KONKKA, *A Fool's Paradise.*

GEORGE KONRÁD, *The City Builder.*

TADEUSZ KONWICKI, *A Minor Apocalypse.*
The Polish Complex.

ANNA KORDZAIA-SAMADASHVILI, *Me, Margarita.*

MENIS KOUMANDAREAS, *Koula.*

ELAINE KRAF, *The Princess of 72nd Street.*

JIM KRUSOE, *Iceland.*

AYSE KULIN, *Farewell: A Mansion in Occupied Istanbul.*

EMILIO LASCANO TEGUI, *On Elegance While Sleeping.*

ERIC LAURRENT, *Do Not Touch.*

VIOLETTE LEDUC, *La Bâtarde.*

EDOUARD LEVÉ, *Autoportrait.*
Newspaper.
Suicide.
Works.

MARIO LEVI, *Istanbul Was a Fairy Tale.*

DEBORAH LEVY, *Billy and Girl.*

JOSÉ LEZAMA LIMA, *Paradiso.*

ROSA LIKSOM, *Dark Paradise.*

OSMAN LINS, *Avalovara.*
The Queen of the Prisons of Greece.

FLORIAN LIPUŠ, *The Errors of Young Tjaž.*

GORDON LISH, *Peru.*

ALF MACLOCHLAINN, *Out of Focus.*
Past Habitual.

The Corpus in the Library.

RON LOEWINSOHN, *Magnetic Field(s).*

YURI LOTMAN, *Non-Memoirs.*

D. KEITH MANO, *Take Five.*

MINA LOY, *Stories and Essays of Mina Loy.*

MICHELINE AHARONIAN MARCOM,
A Brief History of Yes.
The Mirror in the Well.

BEN MARCUS, *The Age of Wire and String.*

WALLACE MARKFIELD, *Teitlebaum's Window.*

DAVID MARKSON, *Reader's Block.*
Wittgenstein's Mistress.

CAROLE MASO, *AVA.*

HISAKI MATSUURA, *Triangle.*

LADISLAV MATEJKA & KRYSTYNA POMORSKA, EDS., *Readings in Russian Poetics: Formalist & Structuralist Views.*

HARRY MATHEWS, *Cigarettes.*
The Conversions.
The Human Country.
The Journalist.
My Life in CIA.
Singular Pleasures.
The Sinking of the Odradek.
Stadium.
Tlooth.

HISAKI MATSUURA, *Triangle.*

DONAL MCLAUGHLIN, *beheading the virgin mary, and other stories.*

JOSEPH MCELROY, *Night Soul and Other Stories.*

ABDELWAHAB MEDDEB, *Talismano.*

GERHARD MEIER, *Isle of the Dead.*

HERMAN MELVILLE, *The Confidence-Man.*

AMANDA MICHALOPOULOU, *I'd Like.*

STEVEN MILLHAUSER, *The Barnum Museum.*
In the Penny Arcade.

RALPH J. MILLS, JR., *Essays on Poetry.*

MOMUS, *The Book of Jokes.*

CHRISTINE MONTALBETTI, *The Origin of Man.*
Western.

FOR A FULL LIST OF PUBLICATIONS, VISIT: www.dalkeyarchive.com

NICHOLAS MOSLEY, *Accident.*
Assassins.
Catastrophe Practice.
A Garden of Trees.
Hopeful Monsters.
Imago Bird.
Inventing God.
Look at the Dark.
Metamorphosis.
Natalie Natalia.
Serpent.

WARREN MOTTE, *Fables of the Novel:*
French Fiction since 1990.
Fiction Now: The French Novel in the
21st Century.
Mirror Gazing.
Oulipo: A Primer of Potential Literature.

GERALD MURNANE, *Barley Patch.*
Inland.

YVES NAVARRE, *Our Share of Time.*
Sweet Tooth.

DOROTHY NELSON, *In Night's City.*
Tar and Feathers.

ESHKOL NEVO, *Homesick.*

WILFRIDO D. NOLLEDO, *But for*
the Lovers.

BORIS A. NOVAK, *The Master of*
Insomnia.

FLANN O'BRIEN, *At Swim-Two-Birds.*
The Best of Myles.
The Dalkey Archive.
The Hard Life.
The Poor Mouth.
The Third Policeman.

CLAUDE OLLIER, *The Mise-en-Scène.*
Wert and the Life Without End.

PATRIK OUŘEDNÍK, *Europeana.*
The Opportune Moment, 1855.

BORIS PAHOR, *Necropolis.*

FERNANDO DEL PASO, *News from*
the Empire.
Palinuro of Mexico.

ROBERT PINGET, *The Inquisitory.*
Mahu or The Material.
Trio.

MANUEL PUIG, *Betrayed by Rita*
Hayworth.

The Buenos Aires Affair.
Heartbreak Tango.

RAYMOND QUENEAU, *The Last Days.*
Odile.
Pierrot Mon Ami.
Saint Glinglin.

ANN QUIN, *Berg.*
Passages.
Three.
Tripticks.

ISHMAEL REED, *The Free-Lance*
Pallbearers.
The Last Days of Louisiana Red.
Ishmael Reed: The Plays.
Juice!
The Terrible Threes.
The Terrible Twos.
Yellow Back Radio Broke-Down.

JASIA REICHARDT, *15 Journeys Warsaw*
to London.

JOÃO UBALDO RIBEIRO, *House of the*
Fortunate Buddhas.

JEAN RICARDOU, *Place Names.*

RAINER MARIA RILKE,
The Notebooks of Malte Laurids Brigge.

JULIÁN RÍOS, *The House of Ulysses.*
Larva: A Midsummer Night's Babel.
Poundemonium.

ALAIN ROBBE-GRILLET, *Project for a*
Revolution in New York.
A Sentimental Novel.

AUGUSTO ROA BASTOS, *I the Supreme.*

DANIËL ROBBERECHTS, *Arriving in*
Avignon.

JEAN ROLIN, *The Explosion of the*
Radiator Hose.

OLIVIER ROLIN, *Hotel Crystal.*

ALIX CLEO ROUBAUD, *Alix's Journal.*

JACQUES ROUBAUD, *The Form of*
a City Changes Faster, Alas, Than the
Human Heart.
The Great Fire of London.
Hortense in Exile.
Hortense Is Abducted.
Mathematics: The Plurality of Worlds of
Lewis.
Some Thing Black.

RAYMOND ROUSSEL, *Impressions of Africa.*

VEDRANA RUDAN, *Night.*

PABLO M. RUIZ, *Four Cold Chapters on the Possibility of Literature.*

GERMAN SADULAEV, *The Maya Pill.*

TOMAŽ ŠALAMUN, *Soy Realidad.*

LYDIE SALVAYRE, *The Company of Ghosts.*
The Lecture.
The Power of Flies.

LUIS RAFAEL SÁNCHEZ, *Macho Camacho's Beat.*

SEVERO SARDUY, *Cobra & Maitreya.*

NATHALIE SARRAUTE, *Do You Hear Them?*
Martereau.
The Planetarium.

STIG SÆTERBAKKEN, *Siamese.*
Self-Control.
Through the Night.

ARNO SCHMIDT, *Collected Novellas.*
Collected Stories.
Nobodaddy's Children.
Two Novels.

ASAF SCHURR, *Motti.*

GAIL SCOTT, *My Paris.*

DAMION SEARLS, *What We Were Doing and Where We Were Going.*

JUNE AKERS SEESE,
Is This What Other Women Feel Too?

BERNARD SHARE, *Inish.*
Transit.

VIKTOR SHKLOVSKY, *Bowstring.*
Literature and Cinematography.
Theory of Prose.
Third Factory.
Zoo, or Letters Not about Love.

PIERRE SINIAC, *The Collaborators.*

KJERSTI A. SKOMSVOLD,
The Faster I Walk, the Smaller I Am.

JOSEF ŠKVORECKÝ, *The Engineer of Human Souls.*

GILBERT SORRENTINO, *Aberration of Starlight.*
Blue Pastoral.
Crystal Vision.

Imaginative Qualities of Actual Things.
Mulligan Stew. Red the Fiend.
Steelwork.
Under the Shadow.

MARKO SOSIČ, *Ballerina, Ballerina.*

ANDRZEJ STASIUK, *Dukla.*
Fado.

GERTRUDE STEIN, *The Making of Americans.*
A Novel of Thank You.

LARS SVENDSEN, *A Philosophy of Evil.*

PIOTR SZEWC, *Annihilation.*

GONÇALO M. TAVARES, *A Man: Klaus Klump.*
Jerusalem.
Learning to Pray in the Age of Technique.

LUCIAN DAN TEODOROVICI,
Our Circus Presents...

NIKANOR TERATOLOGEN, *Assisted Living.*

STEFAN THEMERSON, *Hobson's Island.*
The Mystery of the Sardine.
Tom Harris.

TAEKO TOMIOKA, *Building Waves.*

JOHN TOOMEY, *Sleepwalker.*

DUMITRU TSEPENEAG, *Hotel Europa.*
The Necessary Marriage.
Pigeon Post.
Vain Art of the Fugue.

ESTHER TUSQUETS, *Stranded.*

DUBRAVKA UGRESIC, *Lend Me Your Character.*
Thank You for Not Reading.

TOR ULVEN, *Replacement.*

MATI UNT, *Brecht at Night.*
Diary of a Blood Donor.
Things in the Night.

ÁLVARO URIBE & OLIVIA SEARS, EDS.,
Best of Contemporary Mexican Fiction.

ELOY URROZ, *Friction.*
The Obstacles.

LUISA VALENZUELA, *Dark Desires and the Others.*
He Who Searches.

PAUL VERHAEGHEN, *Omega Minor.*

BORIS VIAN, *Heartsnatcher.*

LLORENÇ VILLALONGA, *The Dolls' Room.*

TOOMAS VINT, *An Unending Landscape.*

ORNELA VORPSI, *The Country Where No One Ever Dies.*

AUSTRYN WAINHOUSE, *Hedyphagetica.*

CURTIS WHITE, *America's Magic Mountain.*
The Idea of Home.
Memories of My Father Watching TV.
Requiem.

DIANE WILLIAMS,
Excitability: Selected Stories.
Romancer Erector.

DOUGLAS WOOLF, *Wall to Wall.*
Ya! & John-Juan.

JAY WRIGHT, *Polynomials and Pollen.*
The Presentable Art of Reading Absence.

PHILIP WYLIE, *Generation of Vipers.*

MARGUERITE YOUNG, *Angel in the Forest.*
Miss MacIntosh, My Darling.

REYOUNG, *Unbabbling.*

VLADO ŽABOT, *The Succubus.*

ZORAN ŽIVKOVIĆ , *Hidden Camera.*

LOUIS ZUKOFSKY, *Collected Fiction.*

VITOMIL ZUPAN, *Minuet for Guitar.*

SCOTT ZWIREN, *God Head.*

AND MORE . . .